Hangman's Back

Nine stories of the supernatural

Ghosts from the future, the present and the past jostle together in this collection to scare and sometimes frighten us.

Rovers were down ten men and hadn't brought a substitute. So how could there be an extra player on the field? George Bunnage set out on his motorbike alone. So, who was sitting on the pillion seat? And why? And was the teacher really at his last lesson – a lesson that so gripped the class that not a sound was made throughout the hour?

"Very enjoyable"   *Junior Bookshelf*

"Genuinely ingenious"   *Recent Children's Fiction*

Also available in Fontana Lions

Dennis Hamley

The Shirt Off a Hanged Man's Back

*Nine Stories of
the Supernatural*

Fontana Lions

First published in Great Britain 1984
by André Deutsch Ltd
First published in Fontana Lions 1986
8 Grafton Street, London W1X 3LA

Fontana Lions is an imprint of
Fontana Paperbacks, a division of
the Collins Publishing Group

Printed in Great Britain by
William Collins Sons & Co. Ltd, Glasgow

These stories are for
all the patient people in schools
in Hertfordshire and beyond
who listened attentively to them
as they were reaching their final
drafts and who never held back
in their comments.

Contents

Crossing

George Bunnage leant forward into the wind. His right hand eased the throttle backward and the Suzuki burst forward at 75 miles an hour. The dawn autumnal mist seemed to part before the straight beam of his headlight. Deep cut tyres bit into the wet road. Inside his leathers George was warm and secure; outside, a cold nip in the rushing air worried at his visor and sent a chill round his forehead. Only four miles to go. His mind cast back to the last time he had travelled this road. Exactly a year ago. The same time; the same speed. The same houses, shops, trees; the same turnings, junctions; the same traffic lights. Even, it seemed, the same traffic coming the other way. But surely not the same ending to the journey? Why was he traversing this road again? As the Suzuki urged itself forward, George racked his brains but found no answer. He remembered . . . what? A party till the small hours: then a breakneck ride home. Forty miles to go. In half an hour at that time of night? No trouble. Roaring, bucketing along, master of the smooth motor underneath him. King of the road, he had exulted to himself. I'm King of the road.

But was he now? Though he continued to rack his brains, he just did not know any more. His snug-fitting leathers seemed to grip tighter round his waist as he leant into a right hand bend. Yes, that night a year ago had been one to remember. If only he could remember it; if only the question that over-rode everything else would not keep surging into his mind. How had his journey ended?

And what had forced him back on the road on this the first anniversary?

George braked as he approached a turning to the left; as the Suzuki slowed suddenly the grip round his waist tightened and he seemed to be pulled ever so slightly backwards. Two miles to go. The mists were rising: the day would be fine. A year ago they were closing in for a dull, dark day. Perhaps that was why it had happened. George's mind was so confused that he could not tell any more. There seemed to be some sort of weight on his left shoulder; the grip round his waist was even tighter. He felt very conscious of his own body. The thought crossed his mind that he might be sickening for something.

A mile. Half a mile. A car parked by the road just ahead. Pull out to pass it. Look in the mirror first. George caught his breath. In the mirror: what was it? A view back up the deserted road – yes. But what else? What was behind him? What shadow seemed to be over his shoulder? A trick of light as the sun began to rise?

It must be. The whole affair was ludicrous. Nothing had happened last year in the next quarter of a mile. It had all been in his imagination, and the urge to retrace his steps a year later was absolute lunacy. Very close now. Soon he would see the lights of that pedestrian crossing, deserted at night but still sending out its meaningless message with no one to heed it – red, green, flashing amber. No one to heed it in the early morning – so who cares if the light is red? Straight through it: don't slacken speed.

All right on a bright morning like this. Nearly all right on a dark, dark dawn with the fog coming. Chances are always worth taking when you think you can get away with them. This morning, as they came into view, they were red. Just like last time. But now it was all clear, all deserted.

So, thought George, I'll open the throttle, roar through the lights at eighty and show myself that last -year everything was all right. The grip round his waist, the weight on his shoulder, were stronger than ever. Even as his fingers started turning the throttle he had an urge to look behind him. He fought it. The Suzuki leapt forward.

8

Last year it had been different. Now it came back clearly. Last year he had carried on through the lights, had too late seen a shape step off the pavement, had felt the shock of collision, fought to keep control, righted himself and roared away without looking back, leaving a huddled, bleeding bundle on the road for others to pick up later.

Without looking back. But now, a year later, the urge to look back was too great. Only a snatched, split second look as he turned his head. But what he saw was buried in his mind for the instant he had left to live. To his right he looked straight into burning eyes set in a skull behind a cracked visor resting, weighing down on his shoulder. And he felt the grip of bony hands inside the gauntlets dig harder into his waist and an inexorable pull from behind. And he seemed to see a huddled bundle rise from the road behind him and a standing figure smiling with satisfaction.

At the inquest a verdict of "misadventure" was passed. The deceased had lost control of his vehicle on the wet road; no blame could be attached to anyone. The coroner drew attention to the fact that two fatalities had occurred in the vicinity over the year before. Perhaps it could be classed as an accident "black spot", though what hidden dangers could lurk in so innocent a stretch of suburban road quite defeated him.

Study Skulls

Three unusual things happened in the Easter holidays which concerned Battershaw Comprehensive School. Hardly anyone noticed the third.

At assembly on the first day back the Head spoke of the first two. Not that anyone needed reminding. One had been in all the papers and on TV. A school party had gone abroad over Easter. The coach had been in a pile-up on the autobahn. Twenty children and a teacher had been killed. The Head read out the names of the dead amid total silence except for tearful sniffs from around the Hall.

As if that weren't enough. The new block at the school had been burnt down at the end of the holidays. An accident or deliberate? Who could tell? But the police were combing the wreckage. You could see the burnt-out shell of the prefabricated buildings through the windows of the Hall. And no one was allowed near the ruins.

The third event hadn't quite finished happening by the end of assembly. Alfie Bradd was on his way. Late on his very first day at Battershaw, he was still toiling up the school drive as the thousand or so pupils filed with rare quietness out of the Hall.

Perhaps Alfie could be excused. It was very nearly his first day back in England. His father was a soldier and had just been posted home from Germany. Last term, Alfie had been at an army school near the Rhine. Now he wondered what joining the first year at Battershaw two terms late would be like.

To look at Alfie, you wouldn't think he was the son of a paratrooper. It would take at least ten years of steaks and body-building to make Alfie fit for yomping across country with full pack and self-loading rifle. He was tiny for his years, with a circular face, curly but short fair hair and round-lensed glasses hiding blue eyes which now and again and quite unexpectedly could look at you with disconcerting piercingness.

"He's deep, is Alfie," said aunts and uncles. "He'll surprise us all one day, will Alfie."

But today, the surprises were on him. He was told by the secretary to go to 1G's form room. There he waited in trepidation for the rest of 1G to join him. And someone else as well. For the first time Alfie was to meet Mr Groatsworth.

As the twenty-nine cowed, rather scruffy eleven-year-olds clattered into the classroom and slumped into their desks, Mr Groatsworth gritted the muscles in his long lantern jaw, stroked his scratchy grey chin and with his other hand smoothed his already dead flat, straight and shiny, thinning black hair. Then he looked at the small – even by the undemanding standards of 1G – figure still standing in front of him, its round glasses glinting.

"For God's sake find yourself something to sit on, Bradd. Then sit on it and tell me what you intend to do on Friday afternoons."

Alfie found a desk vacant – the furthest away from the radiators. Then he answered in the only way he could think of.

"Go home," he said.

Alfie was surprised at the laughter. Surely they could go home in this strange new place?

"No, Bradd," said Mr Groatsworth. "I was not referring to your eventual merciful release. Merely that the Head, in his wisdom, has decreed that last period Friday afternoon shall be called 'Elective Session'. That means you can do whatever you like."

Alfie stared.

"Within reason, of course. There are a number of activities offered by different teachers; you choose one and go to it every Friday without fail and God help you if you miss one. That is what we at Battershaw call 'doing whatever you like'. There's a list on the classroom notice board. Make your mind up during break and let me know by dinner-time."

The notice board was about three metres behind Alfie's left shoulder. He spent all his time till break casting covert long-sighted glances at it. However, it remained a typewritten blur and he only made his head ache.

Break came. The scruffy crew surrounding him scrambled for the door, ignoring him completely. Well, he had been told to perform one task and so, being an army child, Alfie was prepared to do it to the best of his ability. He went up to the notice board and studied it hard.

Drama Club. Not his scene. *Archery (in Hall if wet).* The mind boggled. *Extra PE.* Never. *Beginners' Basketball (unless Archery in Hall in which case Library reading).* Well, it would be, wouldn't it. *Poetry.* Who did they think he was? *Study Skulls.* Eh?

Study Skulls.

It didn't go away.

What could it be? Gravedigging? Reading bumps? It sounded intriguing. He cast his eyes down the rest of the list. Nothing else seemed worth it. Study Skulls it would be.

He didn't fancy milling around outside for the rest of break. He stood by the window and looked out at the blackened, angular shell of the burnt-out new block. The desolation was complete and he was rapt in contemplation of it.

"Alfie Bradd?"

The woman's voice sounding behind him had a questioning tone in it.

"Yes, miss," said Alfie automatically and turned round.

There stood a woman in her thirties, with glasses, short black hair, a maroon pinafore dress and a gentle expression.

Her voice sounded Scottish.

"Have you decided which Elective you're going on?" she said.

12

"What?" said Alfie.

"Your Friday afternoon thing."

"Study Skulls," said Alfie.

"Oh, good," said the woman. "You can be in my group. We'll be pleased to welcome you."

Marvellous. Someone was glad to see him at last.

"I'm Mrs Craigie," she continued. "You won't see me again till Friday afternoon. But then you'll see me in the playground and I'll take you to our room. You'll enjoy it."

"But what do we do?" said Alfie.

"You'll enjoy it," she repeated.

The bell went. 1G burst explosively in. Alfie turned away and went to his desk before anyone else could capture it from him. He didn't see Mrs Craigie leave.

At dinner time, he found Mr Groatsworth in the corridor.

"I've decided, sir," he said.

"Decided what, Bradd?"

"About Friday afternoon."

"Oh, yes. Well, what do you intend to favour?"

"Study Skulls," said Alfie.

"I might have known it," said Mr Groatsworth. "Amazing what chaos a simple, uncorrected typing error can cause. *Skills*, Bradd. Study *Skills*. How to turn you into a brilliant research student without the need actually to have a brain. How to give you the perfect excuse for knowing nothing by telling you where to look it up. The twentieth century's answer to the philosopher's stone. Are you still interested?"

Alfie noticed no sarcasm. It all sounded rather good. Better even than gravedigging. And besides, Mrs Craigie had wanted him there.

"Yes, sir," said Alfie.

"Ah, well," said Mr Groatsworth. "I can't stop the march of progress, however hard I try. Amazingly popular, this Study Skills thing. We have two separate groups already. Which do you want to be in?"

"I've already seen the teacher," said Alfie. "I know which group."

"Which one? Mr Blantyre's?"

'No," said Alfie.

"Oh. The other lot."

"Yes."

Well, it must be.

"That's settled that, then," said Mr Groatsworth. "You're not as daft as you look, Alfie."

There were four days to go till Friday. Alfie began to sink into a half-attending routine, sitting at the back, keeping his head down, his nose clean, speaking when spoken to, volunteering nothing, writing when there was no escape, listening only for the change in the teacher's voice which warned that his attention might be required. He seemed to be making no friends. The rest all seemed to have grown up with each other; his arrival had no effect on them.

Mrs Craigie obviously didn't teach his class. Once or twice he thought he saw her, at the end of a corridor, walking into the geography room or out of the music block. But he was never near enough to speak to her.

Friday afternoon came. The first period was over. Noisily 1G departed to Drama, Archery, Beginners' Basketball (it wasn't raining) and even Poetry. Alfie walked quietly into the playground. Noise was all around him; he didn't seem a part of it.

There was Mrs Craigie, standing quietly by the entrance.

"There you are, Alfie," she said. "Follow me."

She turned and, to Alfie's surprise, walked towards the burnt-out new block.

"But miss, we aren't allowed here," Alfie said.

"Just on Friday afternoons we are," she answered and walked through where there was once a door.

Alfie followed. To his left, and to his great surprise, was a door in the wall that was quite intact and undamaged. Mrs Craigie opened it.

"After you, Alfie," she said.

Alfie entered. She followed and quietly closed the door behind her.

There were about twenty pupils in the room; in age they

seemed between eleven and fourteen. They sat at four tables placed informally round the room. They all looked round as Alfie entered and smiled welcomingly at him. There were also six large, freestanding bookcases, the shelves of which were well stocked. The room was hushed like a library; it almost seemed sound-proofed. There was no sign that there had been a fire.

"Welcome to our group, Alfie," said Mrs Craigie.

"Hello, Alfie," "Come to join us, then, Alfie?" "You'll like it in this group, Alfie." "We are the *greatest*." Such were the remarks which swept over him from the occupants of the room. Just ordinary pupils. He didn't know any of their names; he hardly knew any in the school anyway. But some faces looked familiar, so he must have seen them around.

"What do we do?" he said.

"You've come for Study Skulls, haven't you?" said Mrs Craigie.

"Skills." Alfie carefully corrected her.

"We prefer Skulls," said Mrs Craigie. "But it's the same. Finding things out for yourself."

"How?" said Alfie.

"What's in the room besides people?"

"Books," said Alfie.

Which was true. Hundreds.

"Well now, is there anything you want to know about?"

Alfie thought.

"No, not really," he said at length.

"Is there anything you're interested in?"

Alfie thought again.

"No," he had to admit.

"Nothing?"

"No." He felt ashamed.

"All right," said Mrs Craigie, "Where did you live before you came here?"

"Germany," said Alfie. "Dad was in the army."

"And what do you know about Germany?"

Alfie thought. A big Army camp where everybody

15

spoke English because it was self-contained, almost cut off from the rest of the country. Heathland and pine forest. A great river nearby. The autobahn outside the camp. Did he know much about Germany? Not a lot.

"What part of Germany were you in?"

"The north bit. Where all the British Army camps are."

Mrs Craigie looked at him; he lowered his eyes under her gaze.

"All right, Alfie," she said. "Here's what you're going to do. You're going to find all the books you can about Germany. You're going to get everything out of those books that you can find about your part of it. And you're going to put it all together in your own words and write up a piece of work on your part of Germany that will be better than anything else on these shelves because it will be yours. And you'll find so many things come back to you that you'd thought you'd forgotten you'll be amazed. And you'll have done something really to be proud of."

Alfie didn't think that was very likely. However, he started wandering around the bookcases, looking helplessly at the titles. Mrs Craigie now seemed to take no notice of him. He passed round three bookcases. Not a mention of Germany could he find.

"What are you doing, Alfie?"

A girl of thirteen, in a brown check frock, got up from her seat at her table and approached him.

"Looking for a book," he said.

"That's no good," she said, and led him to the card-index. While she showed him how to use the subject catalogue, she said, "I'm Jane Crossley. My brother Tony is over there by the window."

She pointed and Alfie turned to look. Tony, a dark-haired boy of his own age, smiled and raised his hand in greeting.

Alfie sifted through the catalogue cards, noted the books he wanted and their reference numbers. When he looked up, Jane Crossley had melted silently back to her seat.

A few minutes later and he had carried a pile of eight books to a place at one of the tables. He plonked them down and looked at them hopelessly. What was he supposed to do? Read them all? Where would he start? Wouldn't it take years? He began to wish he was doing Beginners' Basketball.

"What's the matter?" said a voice with a trace of a Jamaican accent.

Alfie turned. Next to him sat a boy with a smiling black face and sparkling eyes. He wore a green jersey and looked about a year older than Alfie.

"What am I supposed to do with this lot?" said Alfie.

"Where do you want to start?" said the boy. While Alfie pondered on this question, the boy continued, "I'm Errol Williams. My sister's in the fourth year."

Yes, thought Alfie. I've probably seen her.

Alfie told Errol what he was hoping to do. Errol asked a few questions – what was the name of the camp, the names of nearby towns, did he know any rivers or mountains nearby? And while Alfie answered, Errol was leafing through the indexes of the books, making a list of references for him to start with. Alfie was amazed at how familiar Errol seemed with all these books. He said so.

"You see one index," said Errol, "you see them all."

And he silently returned to his own patient industry.

Alfie looked up at the page references Errol had given him. And he began to take more. He began to note items down on paper and was soon quarrying for what he wanted through all the books. Memories of his recent past life came back to him; he read information that explained things he hadn't known or had always taken for granted. Time flew by. He was taken by surprise when Mrs Craigie's voice said, "Right, that's it for this week. Pack up now. You can leave your work in here till next time, Alfie."

When Alfie came out of his absorption, he looked round the room. Jane, Ronny and Errol smiled at him. So did all those children he didn't know yet – smiled gravely

17

and silently in that hushed, sun-filled room. Mrs Craigie opened the door. Alfie was first out, into the ruined corridor and then into the open air, which hit him with its freshness. He was immediately surrounded by hordes of pupils coming out of the main building. Nobody took any notice of him. He turned to look for the rest of the Study Skulls group. He saw none. They must have gone out a different way or been swallowed up in the crowd while he was still blinking in the sunlight.

Yes, it had been a good afternoon. People who liked him, welcomed him, helped him. He'd learnt a lot. And he'd really concentrated, been taken out of himself. When had that last happened? He couldn't remember.

The weekend passed; the next school week began. Nothing happened in his own class to make him feel at home. He felt withdrawn, out of it all. The teachers seemed to be taking as little notice of him as the pupils did. Mr Groatsworth, however, spoke to him on Monday morning.

"You got to your Elective all right on Friday?" he said.

"Yes, sir," said Alfie.

"After all that, you know, I forgot to put your name on the list for Study Skills group B. They wouldn't have known you were coming."

"But I told you, sir. I saw the teacher," said Alfie.

"So you did. No harm done, then," said Mr Groatsworth and ignored him for the rest of the week.

Alfie didn't worry about that. Everybody else seemed to as well.

During the next week, Alfie looked for his Study Skulls group. He didn't see them. Nor did he see Mrs Craigie. Except perhaps fleetingly – a figure crossing a corridor, framed for an instant in an open doorway; Errol's face for a split second laughing through a window; Jane's brown check skirt swinging away towards the cloakrooms. Alfie called after them, gave chase – never caught up. But by Friday, they were all he wanted to see, all he thought about – almost, all he lived for.

Friday afternoon arrived at last. The period before Study Skulls passed like an age. His heart was thumping with anticipation until the bell went and he was released. Mrs Craigie was in the playground again; he followed her as she walked silently through the milling crowd to the new block and her room. Inside again, here they all were; Jane, Tony, Errol, all the others he didn't know yet but knew he soon would.

When the door was closed, the quiet hush of the room was almost oppressive. Through the windows Alfie could see the rest of the school just a few yards and yet a million miles away. The work on his Germany study was exactly where he had left it the week before. He sat down and drew the books towards him.

As he worked, he became aware that the rest of them had left their tables and were surrounding him. It was as if they wanted to find out what he was doing, to talk to him. And he found he wanted to talk to them. They asked him questions about Germany; he answered them when he could and when he couldn't he looked them up. He began to revel in this, being the centre of attention.

As they spoke he saw something shiny on the floor flash in the sunlight.

"What's that?" he said.

"Go and look, Alfie," said Jane.

Alfie went to it and picked it up. It was an identity bracelet. The name on it was Gary Somervell.

"That's my elder brother," said a boy with tousled hair wearing a blue jersey and jeans. "I'm Simon Somervell."

Alfie made as if to give the bracelet to Simon. He drew back.

"No," he said. "You give it to him, Alfie."

"Why not you?" said Alfie. "He's your brother."

"I don't live with him any more. You keep it and give it to him after school. You don't know anybody here yet and this will give you a chance to get to know my brother."

It must have been because things never seemed quite real in this room that Alfie thought the suggestion perfectly reasonable. Perhaps Gary had left home, or the Somervells had split up, Gary going with one parent, Simon with the other. Best not to ask too much.

"How will I know him?" he said.

"You'll see him outside the gates right after school, talking to Debra Parkes. You can't miss Gary. He looks a bit like me but he's got a red stripe in his hair and he's bound to be smoking a cigarette."

Alfie put the bracelet in his pocket. He wanted to get on with talking to his friends while Mrs Craigie looked placidly on. All too soon the afternoon was at an end and he was once again outside on his own.

Ah, well. He had a job to do.

Just as Simon had said, there was Gary outside the school gates. The red stripe was unmistakable, the expected cigarette dangled from his fingers. The short-haired girl with him was presumably Debra Parkes. Gary was very large and forbidding. Alfie took the bracelet out of his pocket. It didn't seem to shine as it had in the Study Skulls room. It was dirty, discoloured. Still, Simon had asked him to give it back to Gary and give it back he would, even if Gary did look like Dracula.

"Excuse me," he said. "Is this yours?"

Gary snatched it from him and looked at it. Then he fixed Alfie with a furious stare.

"Where did you get this," he hissed.

"It was in Mrs Craigie's room," said Alfie. "Your brother Simon asked me to give it to you."

The effect on Gary was amazing. He turned dead white; for a moment Alfie thought he was going to faint. Debra, her eyes fixed on Alfie, put her arms out to steady Gary; he recovered and shook her off. Then he pushed his face towards Alfie.

"You're cracked, mate," he said. "You're bloody cracked."

He turned on his heel and ran. Debra followed him, trying hard to keep up. Alfie watched them as Gary pushed his way through young children waiting for buses and getting on bicycles and disappeared round a corner, closely pursued by Debra.

He shrugged his shoulders.

"Funny bloke," he said out loud.

Monday was remarkable as being the first day on which anyone at Battershaw except Mr Groatsworth and the Study Skulls team had spoken to him without a reason to do with work. And Alfie wished it wasn't.

Gary Somervell grabbed him by the back of the collar.

"Right," he said. "What do you think you're playing at?"

He didn't look chalk-white and about to faint today. On the contrary. He was livid.

"I don't know what you mean," croaked Alfie, half choked.

"That load of cobblers about Mrs Craigie's room and my brother. You know something, don't you? What are you after?"

"It's true what I said."

"It *can't* be."

"*It is.*"

Gary let him go. Alfie rubbed his neck.

"It can't be."

Gary's voice was calmer.

"Why shouldn't it be?" said Alfie.

"Oh, come on. You know why not."

Alfie didn't answer. What did Gary mean.

"Show me where you found my bracelet," said Gary.

"No," said Alfie. "Not till Friday afternoon. Mrs Craigie says I can only go in the new block then."

They both looked towards the gutted shell. Alfie thought Gary was going to insist they went there and then. But he didn't.

"All right," he said finally. "When you go on Friday, I'm coming too. Right?"

"Right," said Alfie.

"And don't go trying to shake me off."

21

"I won't," said Alfie.

"You're cracked, mate," said Gary. "And so must I be to go with you. But if you're having me on I'll kill you."

And he walked off.

On Tuesday morning, after registration, Mr Groatsworth called Alfie to him.

"Why did you tell me you'd been to Study Skills group B?" he said.

"Because I have, sir."

"Come on, Alfie. Don't lie to me. You didn't go the first time when you said you had and you certainly didn't go on Friday because they were expecting you."

"But I *did*," said Alfie. "I *did*. I'm doing some work on Germany."

"I'm not taking any action, Alfie, because you're new here. But you get yourself to Study Skills group B on Friday or I'll skin you alive, or put you in detention. Whichever is the more painful."

"But I *did* go," said Alfie.

"You'd better not say any more," said Mr Groatsworth. "Or you and I might fall out. I don't want to get angry with you."

From now until Friday, Alfie could concentrate on nothing. Round and round and round his mind went, worrying away at three things. Why should Mrs Craigie say he'd not been to Study Skills when she took him there herself? Why should Gary think he was cracked just because he'd given his bracelet back? Why was Gary scared at first? And then why was he angry? Even if they did live apart now, Gary and Simon must see each other during the day at school.

These people at Battershaw were the weirdest lot he'd ever met. Unfriendly, scared and angry by turns, unwelcoming. Even his Study Skulls group acted like they were from another world.

He was musing thus on Thursday afternoon when he felt a jab with an elbow in his ribs. It was Gerry Forman, who sat in the next row.

"You'd better be at Study Skills on Friday," he said. "You won't half cop it if you don't. Groatsworth'll hit the roof it he hears you're missing again."

Alfie stared at him.

"You aren't in the group," he said.

"'Course I am," said Gerry. "Been in it since we started this caper. They kicked up a right fuss when you never turned up last week after Groatsworth said you'd be there."

"But I've not missed one yet," said Alfie.

Gerry gave him a peculiar look and turned away.

Alfie couldn't sleep on Thursday night. Something strange was happening and he didn't know what it was. He lay awake hour after hour looking at the ceiling. The same questions crossed and recrossed his mind. And in front of his eyes he saw the faces of the Study Skulls group. Jane, Tony, Errol, Simon, Mrs Craigie and the rest. All smiling in that unruffled way they seemed to share.

Why did they smile like that? Why was it so important *he* gave the bracelet to Gary? Why was he so happy with them? Why could he concentrate, think, work with them when he couldn't anywhere else? And he thought about what he did in the Study Skulls group. His German study. And how doing it made him relive his past life, so clear were the impressions he received as he sorted out and arranged his material. His thoughts drifted away to memories of that life. And to one thing in particular so recent he'd not thought of it before. The last night of all, before they left for good just before Easter. Sergeant Bradd had picked up his new Ford Escort with right-hand drive from a local garage. He was delighted because his personal export arrangements would save over a thousand pounds on the price he would have paid in England. And he and Alfie drove back to the army camp along the autobahn. It was growing dark; there was a grey, misty drizzle. Cars, lorries, coaches overtook them, engine noises rising towards them and falling away as they passed, headlights blazing in the murk as Sergeant Bradd slowly got used to his brand new car. And then . . . Here Alfie's memory failed him. *Something* happened. What was it? It eluded him. But it was vital he remembered, because it seemed in an obscure way to have something to do with the Study Skulls group. What was it? What was it?

As dawn approached, there came a feeling that was new to him. Fear.

The fear stayed with Alfie all morning. It was like an involuntary shiver that seemed to start in his stomach and move into his legs and shoulders. He tried very hard to control it but was sure his shaking was obvious to anybody who looked at him hard. Nobody did though, so nobody noticed. For once, Alfie did not want the time until Study Skulls to pass quickly. Maths, history, French – now they shot past while he wanted them to stay as comfortable capsules of time he could curl up inside before being pitched out to a meeting with the inscrutable Mrs Craigie.

But the moment arrived. He nearly dodged it to follow Gerry Forman off to Study Skills Group B. But he thought again and went to his normal spot.

Gary was there already, pacing up and down impatiently. In the dull, sunless atmosphere his red streak looked as if it had been applied with day-glo paint.

He scowled when he saw Alfie.

"For a minute I thought you weren't coming," he muttered.

"I'm here," said Alfie.

"She's not," said Gary. "I knew she wouldn't be."

"Yes, she is," said Alfie. "She's behind you."

Alfie hadn't seen Mrs Craigie approach. But she was there, as if she had been waiting patiently all afternoon.

Gary turned. He too saw Mrs Craigie. His face went chalk-white, just as it had when Alfie had given him the bracelet. He staggered slightly as if he had been hit. Then he turned to Alfie. But he said nothing.

"Come on, Gary," said Mrs Craigie's soft voice. "We're all here to see you again."

24

She led the way to the new block and the Study Skulls room. Alfie followed as he always did. Gary came as well, unwillingly, as if being pulled along by an invisible rope.

They entered the room. As always, it was hushed, quiet. The twenty children at their tables turned to the new arrivals. They all smiled in the calm, serene way Alfie knew so well.

Gary seemed to lean into him, as if seeking support.

"Christ," he muttered.

"I told you, didn't I?" said Alfie.

Simon came forward.

"Hullo, Gary," he said. "So Alfie gave you the bracelet."

Gary looked at him without saying a word.

"We saw you leave it in here," said Simon. "You came here into our room and we watched you. You dropped it and didn't know. You shouldn't have come in here that night. There was no need to."

Gary turned haggard eyes on his brother. Now he did speak. He shrieked at the top of his voice.

"There wasn't anybody here. There couldn't have been."

"We watched you," repeated Simon quietly.

"You bloody well couldn't have." Gary was still shrieking. "It was pitch dark. And the room was empty. And it was a whole week after . . . after . . ."

Mrs Craigie spoke.

"Gary," she said, "we wanted you back here to tell you. We had to tell you. It was nobody's fault. We know what you felt. But you couldn't get revenge by doing what you did."

Gary turned on her.

"Yes I could," he shouted. "It was all your fault, you silly bloody cow. It was all because of you. *You made it all happen*. If my brother Simon hadn't listened to you he wouldn't have been . . . have been . . ."

"Yes, Gary?" said Mrs Craigie.

"I can't say it," said Gary.

25

"You have to say it," said Mrs Craigie. "If you'd said it and admitted it to start with you wouldn't have done what you did. And we wouldn't have had to stay here waiting in our room until you came to us and we could tell you."

Alfie looked from one to the other as this mystifying conversation took place – mystifying in both what it said and how it sounded. Gary's voice, shrieking, hoarsely whispering, as his feelings seemed to rip at his throat like tearing cloth, was immediate, filling Alfie's ears from a mere handslength away. But Mrs Craigie and Simon were remote, even, measured – just as voices always were in that room.

He turned to the table where his work lay, untouched from last week. Germany. His life there. Everything that had happened over the years out of Britain – ending with the last night and the drive down the autobahn in the brand new Escort. He thought of it again, just as he had remembered it the night before. And there was that something else – something that was very important, something just out of the range of his memory. What was it? He wrinkled his forehead with the effort of recall, bent his head and drew his books towards him. Then he sat up again. Sitting in a row, facing him, were the four he knew best. Jane, Tony, Errol, Simon.

Then his mind clicked and even more clearly than before he was back in the Escort, strapped in to the passenger seat, smelling the cloth and plastic newness.

"Why don't you do more than fifty, Dad?" he had said. "Everybody's overtaking us."

"I want this car home in England in one piece," said Sergeant Bradd. "And us with it. The others can go as fast as they like. That's their look out."

He was keeping to the inside lane. He winced as a Porsche screamed past at over twice the speed of the Escort.

"That fellow won't last long," he said.

A huge container lorry, travelling nearly as fast as the Porsche, blasted its way down the outer lane and swung into the inside lane in front of them. It was making way for a BMW which also disappeared into the drizzly dusk.

"They're all mad," said Sergeant Bradd.

Another vehicle passed them in the outer lane; like the lorry, it turned into the inside lane to let a faster car through. It was a twenty-five seater coach and for a while it stayed immediately in front of the Bradd's Escort. Faces looked down on the Escort from the rear window. In the car headlights and the glow of the sodium lamps lighting up the autobahn, their features could be seen clearly. Alfie relived the moment with absolute clarity.

The faces were those of Jane, Tony, Errol and Simon. They smiled down on the Escort and waved. Alfie waved back. He felt somehow that a message had passed between them, but he could not say what it was.

The left-hand winker of the coach started flashing. The coach pulled out past the container lorry and accelerated quickly away down the outer lane.

"He wants to be careful as well," said Sergeant Bradd. "It's a slippery, misty evening."

They left the autobahn at the next exit. The following day they started back for England.

In the Study Skulls room Alfie stared again at the four faces still smiling in front of him, in the same order he had seen them through the window of the coach. And here they all were in the burnt-out new block. But it wasn't burnt out. Yes, it was. It must be.

The fear that had fluttered all round Alfie's body that day suddenly concentrated itself inside his mind. Where was he? Who were these people? What was he doing here? What was this strange scene before him where it seemed as though Gary was being brought to judgement?

"Now Gary," said Mrs Craigie. "You know what you did and why you did it. We saw you." Her voice sounded immensely patient. "We were all here in my room. We had all met in here before we left for the Easter trip to Germany. We all assembled in here so I could check everyone before we went out to the coach. You saw us

27

here, Gary. You were there with all the mums and dads and brothers and sisters to wave us away. So after it all happened we came back here to watch because we knew what you would do."

"You took my brother away," said Gary. "We'll never see him again."

"Not me, Gary," said Mrs Craigie. "I didn't make the coach crash."

Alfie suddenly felt dizzy.

Mrs Craigie now seemed to remember him.

"Let Alfie decide," she said. "Let Alfie see what happened. Come with us, Alfie."

Alfie now tried to jerk himself away. But Jane, Tony, Errol and Simon stood up and reached out towards him. He felt their touch – light, cold on his wrists. And he had to stand up with them, whether he liked it or not.

"We can take you back, Alfie," said Jane. "You'll see what we saw."

Suddenly, the room was dark and empty. Outside the window street-lights beyond the deserted bulk of the main school shone yellow. Alfie seemed a spectator, one of an invisible crowd waiting expectantly.

All at once, there was a shattering crash. One of the windows had been broken. More crashes; someone was knocking all the glass out of the pane. Something large and heavy was thrown through and clattered noisily to the floor. A figure scrambled in across the window sill. It was unrecognisable. It moved to a table. There was a scratch and a spurt of flame as a match was lit. By the quick, tiny light, Alfie saw who it was – Gary. He bent down as if looking for something with the light of the match – the object he had thrown through the window. He found it and picked it up. It was a sledgehammer.

Alfie could hear Gary's breathing in the darkness after the match had gone out. The breathing turned into a whispering which grew louder and more impassioned.

"I'd kill the bitch if she were here. I'd kill her; I'd kill her."

28

And he started swinging the sledgehammer so that it crashed down on tables, chairs and bookcases; the swinging and the crashing and the splintering and the chanting became a rhythm; "I'd *kill* her, I'd *kill* her, I'd *kill* her."

Wood cracked; tables and chairs broke; books littered the room. The moon outside rose as Gary went about his destruction.

Then he stopped. He stooped and picked up a book. He looked at it sullenly. Then he ripped off its cover and began to tear out pages. The book was soon destroyed; pages fluttered round the room. He picked up another and did the same. And another. As he did so he began to shout again.

"I'll get the woman . . . I'll get the school . . . bastard school . . . bastard woman . . . killed Simon. I'll make them pay."

At length, he stopped. The room was a complete wreck. Out of breath, he looked around.

"That'll do to start with," he said. "I'll pay them back. I'll get all the revenge I can." His voice rose again to a shout at the empty air.

"I'm doing it for you, Simon."

Then he leant back up against the windowsill over which he had entered and took a packet of cigarettes out of his pocket. He struck another match and lit one. He threw the match to the ground; it fell among some loose pages. He took a few drags at his cigarette. Then, convulsively, he threw it away, picked up his sledgehammer, hurled it through the window and scrambled after it. As he hoisted himself up, something fell to the ground with a tiny tinkle. An identity bracelet.

In the empty room, little fingers of smoke from the match and the half-finished cigarette felt their way round the loose pages of the destroyed books. They began to smoulder; a breeze through the broken window fanned them. Gradually but inexorably a fire spread.

The room lightened. It was intact again and as Alfie had

always known it. Mrs Craigie stood in front of him once again.

"Well, Alfie?" she said.

"He did it for Simon," said Alfie.

"Why?"

"For revenge."

"For what?"

Yes, for what? For what unspeakable things?

"Come with us again," said Mrs Craigie. "See things through our eyes again."

The cold touch of Jane, Tony, Errol and Simon was still on him. But the surroundings were different. He was with them on the back seat of the coach. The autobahn unwound itself behind them; they were travelling fast. The four talked, laughed, sang. Alfie did not listen; instead, he watched the familiar road. He saw a Porsche overtake at well over a hundred miles an hour; a BMW nearly as fast. The coach then pulled out into the fast lane – but only for a moment as an Audi came speeding up from behind. Back the coach went into the inside lane, slipping in just in front of a Ford Escort.

The four looked down on it with interest.

"Ford Escort," said Simon.

"What a little driver," said Jane. "He can hardly see out of the windscreen."

"Don't be daft," said Tony. "It's right-hand drive. It must be English."

"There's a man driving it," said Errol. "That must be his kid with him. He's got glasses on."

"I wonder if they're going home to England like us," said Jane. "Perhaps we'll see him there."

"He won't be going to Battershaw if he's got any sense," said Simon.

They waved down at the tiny figure in the passenger seat. It waved back. Then the coach pulled out again, overtaking a big container lorry.

"He might be back home before us," said Jane. "We should have given him a message to take. We could have blown on the windows and done mirror writing."

30

"What sort of messages?" said Tony.

"That we're all OK, that we've had a great time and we'll be back in a few days."

"They know that already," said Errol.

The coach passed the next exit from the autobahn. The speed did not slacken. By now, the container lorry was behind them in the outside lane. The drizzle and mist seemed to be getting worse.

"Miss," called out Jane. "We've just passed an English car. There was a boy sitting in the front. We thought we'd try and send him a message in case he got home before us."

Mrs Craigie turned round from her seat in the front.

"No need, Jane," she said. "We'll be home on Wednesday."

There was a sudden loud scream of brakes and a violent deceleration which knocked them sprawling out of their seats and onto the floor. The coach skidded wildly and then crashed into the cars ahead which in turn had ploughed into a lorry which had shed its load in front of them. There was a rending crash from behind as the container lorry drove helplessly into the coach. The pile-up was complete.

Alfie was in the room again. He hardly dared look round. But all was as usual.

"It was no one's fault," said Mrs Craigie.

"See, Alfie," said Jane. "We did give you a message, didn't we? We called you here to get Gary so he'd know it wasn't Mrs Craigie's fault. Nobody found his bracelet but you."

Gary was slumped in a corner of the room, sobbing. Simon spoke to him.

"I've gone from you, Gary," he said. "There's nothing you can do about it. Breaking Mrs Craigie's room up doesn't help."

"I didn't mean to burn the place down," said Gary. "I'm sorry, Simon."

"Goodbye, Gary," said Simon.

"Goodbye, Alfie," said all twenty pupils together.

Mrs Craigie laid a cold finger on Alfie's forehead as he stood with head bowed.

"Goodbye, Alfie," she said. "Don't ever forget what you did in Study Skulls."

Alfie looked up. Except for Gary, there was no one there. The room they stood in was a gutted shell. The wind murmured through the windowless frames and the blackened steel girders of the wrecked building. The tables, the books, the project on Germany were all gone.

Alfie looked at Gary.

"You burned the new block down," he said.

"You saw," said Gary. "I didn't mean to. I was angry. I didn't know what I was doing."

"What will you do now?" said Alfie.

"I don't know," said Gary.

Suddenly, Alfie felt an enormous wave of sympathy for Gary. His brother had suffered a pointless death and the need to hit out at someone or something was too great.

"I won't tell," he said.

"I will," said Gary, standing up. "Simon wants me to. Don't you see? Police crawling all over this place and none of them finding the bracelet? Simon took care of that."

"What will happen to you?" said Alfie.

"God knows," said Gary. "I'll have to take my chance."

And he walked out of the new block with dignified resolution.

Alfie was left on his own. A feeling of relief swept over him. Now he could begin to live properly at Battershaw. Groatsworth wasn't so bad. Next week he'd be in Study Skills group B and Gerry Forman might prove a good mate. There'd be some way to square Groatsworth over this Friday's absence.

And Gary? Gary would never forget him.

And he himself would never forget Mrs Craigie. Or Jane, Tony, Errol, Simon and the rest. He would never see them again – but they would always be with him. His first friends at Battershaw. And all they taught him – it would be with him for ever.

Study Skulls.

No. In future he had to get it right. Study *Skills*.

But he preferred Study Skulls.

The Substitute

He didn't wait for the coach to stop as it passed the end of
his road. He was standing at the door, sports bag in one
hand, the other hand clinging on to the rail, and stepped
nimbly off.

"Cheers," he shouted and gave a thumbs-up sign to the
rest of the team. A last combined chant of "*We* are the
great-est" sounded through the open windows of the coach
as the others waved back. And then he was alone.

He was eighteen and dead lucky to be in the Rovers first
team. All right, it was only the South-east Midlands
League. But Rovers were classed as a Senior club now.
Next season they'd play in the FA Vase and could even
get to Wembley. You never knew. And after a win like
today's! How could anybody ever have had an experience
like it?

A little voice at the back of his mind said, "Don't think
too hard about it. You might not like what you find." He
silenced the voice. "We won, didn't we?" he said aloud
and opened the front door of his house.

He'd had a shower back at the Pakenham Town
ground; a spruce-up, something to eat and he'd be
meeting Sandra by eight o'clock. Meanwhile, he had to
tell somebody about this extraordinary game.

His father was sitting in front of the television. I bet he's
been there all afternnon, he thought. Twenty years ago he
was playing for the Rovers himself. And there's men older
than him still turn out regularly. I hope I don't end up
limp and hopeless like that.

"How did you get on, then, son?"

"We won, Dad. We won. 4–3. But it was *weird*."

"You went one better than we did twenty-five years ago, then."

"We're in the semi-finals of the County Senior Cup. I can't believe it."

"We could have made it, too," said his father. "If all of us old boys could be twenty years younger we'd give you three goals start and then a good run-around."

"You ought to give us a bit of support, Dad. You ought to come and watch us. We're worth supporting, you know."

"No, not now. I've not got the heart for it. A few cans of beer, my chair in front of the telly and switching between 'Grandstand' and 'World of Sport' is my idea of a good Saturday afternoon nowadays."

"But look what we've done. We went all the way to Pakenham for the replay. We nearly lost at home; we were lucky to draw. And we were three-nil down half-an-hour from the end today. *And we won* 4–3. That's *fantastic!*"

"It was because you had a replay at Pakenham that I wouldn't come," said his father. A look almost of pain crossed his face. His son didn't notice.

"I tell you, Dad, it really was *weird*. I didn't fancy our chances in the replay. And Fred Akers never turned up: we only had eleven players. No substitute when we needed one. We should have got hammered."

His father seemed not to listen: he was starting on his own story.

"The last time Rovers played Pakenham Town in the County Cup and took them to a replay was twenty-five years ago. We drew with them at home, just like you did. But we never got to the replay. Have I ever told you why?"

His son carried on without taking any notice. He was too full of his own amazing experience.

"We started playing like idiots. Pakenham were all over us. Thirty minutes to go and we were three-nil down. And we deserved it. It was a carve-up. Then poor old Joe

Farmer got carried off on a stretcher. We thought he'd broken his leg. So did he. He didn't half shout. But he's all right. So there we were. Ten men and no substitute. Pakenham should have scored fifteen."

He paused for breath and his father spoke again.

"Have I ever mentioned the name Ronny Willard to you? I'll never forget Ronny. He was sixteen and played like a dream. Seeing him with us was like roast turkey on a plate of corned beef. We must have seemed a bunch of country scrubbers to him. He wasn't staying here long. All the big clubs were after him. He'd already signed apprentice forms for Manchester United and as soon as the season ended he was going up there to club lodgings. After all – well, we'd all have heard about him again. He'd have played for England for sure. He was magic."

"Come on, Dad; it's today you want to worry about, not all those years ago. The miracle happened today."

"No, I'll never forget Ronny Willard."

"Dad, listen, will you? We were three-nil down and only ten men. But then it started being peculiar. It's like Pakenham started chasing shadows. I can't decribe it. I can only say what I saw. You know how you get the ball, turn quick because there's someone on you, see one of your own team and push the ball out to him without thinking who it is? Well, that's what happened to me. I got the ball; the Pakenham number 4 was crowding me. I looked up, saw this bloke in a red shirt haring down the right – and I was just going to pass to him. Then I saw he'd taken a couple of defenders with him. So I pushed the ball back to Kevin Rafferty. Well, Kevin had a clear run of the goal. And he scored. Half the Pakenham defence was on the wrong side of the field. None of our lads with them. Who had they been chasing? I don't know. But they didn't half start arguing among themselves. Well, that was the first one we pulled back. Mind if I have one of your cans of beer?"

He picked one up and pulled the ring. His father did likewise and continued dreamily.

"I remember Ronny had left school. He'd got himself a job in a builder's yard to tide him over until Man United wanted him. So he could have the whole season with us. That was our best season for years."

He poured his beer into a glass and took a long swallow. His son looked at him irritably.

"You're not listening to a word I'm saying, are you? You're missing something fantastic. Our next goal was a penalty. And it was a real laugh. Their number 5 was a clogger. If the ref had had any sense he'd have booked him long before. Anyway, there he was elbowing his way around in the penalty area just as Charlie Simms was bursting through. Now for a split second I thought there was one of our lads in the box being marked by the number 5. So did he because he leant into him while the ref wasn't looking to knock him off balance. But there was no one there to give a dig to. It was the number 5 who lost his balance. Sprawled right into Charlie just as he was going to shoot. Well, the ref gave a penalty. What else could he do? You had to laugh. The number 5 never meant to foul Charlie. But where was the one he *did* foul? Dad, *listen*."

But his father looked deep into the clear brown beer in his glass as if he could see the past in it.

"Yes, it was our best season ever. We were top of the old district league – we hadn't got big ideas in those days like you have. And we were in the fifth round of the County Cup. We'd never got beyond round three before. And we were drawn at home to Pakenham Town."

The son, ignoring him, went on, as if he had to spill his story out or burst, whether anybody listened or not.

"This is the most incredible bit. The equaliser was the daftest goal of the lot. The number 5 was in a right state by now and we were putting a lot of pressure on him. He had to pass back to the goalkeeper. Soft pass along the ground – no danger; none of us could get near it by then. But I could have sworn I saw one of our lads charging in from nowhere as if he was going to thump it. The goalie moved out to cover where he thought the shot would go. But there was no one there. So he was stranded over one side of the goal and the ball just trickled in the net on the other. Pakenham were furious. They were arguing among themselves worse than ever. We were laughing our heads off. It really was like they were chasing shadows and we were watching them. Even the ref noticed something and before they kicked off again he counted us, just to make sure. But there were only ten on our side. You're not taking a word of this in, are you, Dad?"

No, he wasn't. His own story was reaching its climax.

"You know, when we played Pakenham we should have won first time. We were all over them – should have had six. But we got none. I don't know why. I hit the bar twice myself. Five minutes from the end we got our only goal. Ronny scored it, of course. Beautiful, it was. Did it all himself, as though he despaired of us. As well he might."

"Yes, well, nobody could despair of us today. Not after our last goal. I scored it. And it was just like the rest. Kevin crossed the ball from the right; the goalie looked to have it covered. Then this red streak seemed to dive at it – like someone running in and making a really spectacular diving header. The goalkeeper fell one way to cover it, the defence turned to get this man of ours – and there was no one there. They all missed the ball and it came straight to me. Open goal – I wasn't going to miss that."

He stopped, to savour again the glory of that moment. And his father started again.

"Two minutes to go twenty-five years ago and we were still one-nil up. We thought Ronny's goal would be enough; we must have slackened off. Anyway, their centre-forward got away; he burst through and shot. Ronny tried to get back to cut the ball off; it had beaten the goalkeeper. And he nearly did it too; he lunged across and somehow got a boot to it. No one else could have come near it. But he didn't divert it quite enough and it was over the line. They'd drawn with us. We had to slog across to their place for a replay. I'll never forget how

38

upset Ronny was. He blamed himself for putting through his own goal. There he sat in the changing-room, crying his eyes out. He took it all to heart so much, did Ronny. We tried to tell him it wasn't his fault but he wouldn't have it. He kept on saying, over and over again. 'I'll get you through the replay. I'll get you through the replay.' I can hear him now. 'I'll get you through the replay.'"

For the first time, the son's attention was jerked away from his own story.

"And did he?"

"No, he never did. That was his last game for us – for anybody. He was working in the builder's yard the day before the replay. The foreman told him to get up on the floor of the wood store to hand some planking down. He shinned up a dodgy ladder and no one was down below supporting it. And it broke with him on the top. Twenty feet he dropped, with nothing to break his fall. He died in hospital that night."

The son stared at his father. The little voice at the back of his mind that he'd silenced as he entered the house came back to him. *Don't think too hard about it.*

"Dad, it's only just registering. After the final whistle today I saw the extra man who'd been playing for us. He was walking off the pitch next to me. And he spoke to me."

But his father was miles away.

"What a waste that was. What a rotten terrible waste. He was magic, was Ronny Willard. We never played the replay. The lads wouldn't. They didn't have the heart to. I told them Ronny would have wanted us to play, but they wouldn't. So he never got us through the replay. Pakenham went into the next round automatically."

"Dad, you've got to listen. This player. He'd got a red shirt on, same as ours. But it was baggy and a bit faded. And his number wasn't printed on in white like ours. It was a big black number stitched in to a white patch on the back of his shirt. But it was a number 12, as if he was the substitute."

His father was listening hard, looking at his son with an odd expression.

"But we didn't have substitutes then," he said.

"Oh, heck, Dad. It's only just sinking in. I was hot and sweating, but next to him I felt icy. And he spoke to me. I swear he spoke to me. 'I said I'd get you through the replay.' I knew what his words were but somehow I didn't hear them. I can't describe it. 'Yes,' I said, and ran on without him. I didn't see him again. And we were so amazed and chuffed about winning he clean slipped out of my mind."

The father took a long and contented swig at his beer and looked gently at his son's pale and frightened face. He spoke.

"I'll never forget Ronny sitting in the changing-room crying his eyes out after the last game. He really took that own goal to heart. I knew he meant what he said."

The Overbalancing Man

If Alison's house had been a hundred metres further down the road she could have travelled free on the school bus. Instead, she had to walk.

The house in which she lived with her parents, her two younger brothers, three dogs, four cats, six rabbits and several hundred battery hens was set back from the road and surrounded by trees. On one side was open farming land. On the other were two fields, the disused railway line and beyond that the town. And the secondary school was right over the other side so – except on the rare occasions her father drove into town and gave her a lift – she had plenty of scope for keeping fit. All the pupils from the villages and outlying farms passed her in the school bus: the first part of her journey there and the last part of her journey back were always made alone.

It was a pleasant journey, none the less. First, the hedge-lined road almost bare of traffic whatever the time of day – it was not one of the main routes into the town. Then over the old level-crossing, where the gates were always shut because no trains came any more – though the rails were still there, rusty and weed-smothered. Just to the left was the deserted, crumbling railway station, right on the very edge of the town.

Once over the level crossing, Alison began to pass houses and meet friends also going to school; more and more of them. Through the town centre they went, past the new shopping precinct, the Town Hall, the library, the hospital and at last to the school.

Coming home, she gradually shed her companions, until, as she approached the old level crossing, she was once again alone. It was a routine: the first and last moments of her school day were quite solitary.

However, one June afternoon in her second year at the secondary school she was suddenly not quite so solitary.

She was walking home. The weather was warm and sunny. The time was 4.25. She was walking over the level-crossing and wondering why nobody had ever removed the rails and tarred over the gaps left in the road when she chanced to look at the abandoned railway station. Its two platforms were still intact, though covered in long weedy grass which had burst through the old asphalt. The overbridge was still there: the station buildings – derelict, vandalised – still stood. But to her knowledge, nobody ever came there.

Until today. For, on the platform on the town side, right at the edge as if he were about to overbalance on to the tracks, stood a man.

Something about his appearance looked strange to Alison. After a moment, she realized what it was. His clothes. He wore a tall hat. His black coat was strangely cut away at the front and appeared to have something like tails behind. And his trousers were narrow and oddly rucked up over his shoes. They seemed to be made of very thick material. He looked like someone out of a fancy dress parade or a television version of a book by Charles Dickens.

Very strange, thought Alison, and bent down to tie her shoelace. When she straightened up, she looked again at the station platform.

The man was gone.

Well, why shouldn't somebody walk round the old place? thought Alison. And I'd put old clothes on as well: it must be filthy in there. So she went home to her parents, brothers and livestock and thought no more of it.

Soon she forgot about him, because for the next four days he was not there.

But on Midsummer's Day itself, as she passed the level-crossing, she chanced to look towards the old platforms and saw him again.

42

He was dressed in exactly the same way – the cutaway, swallowtail jacket, the narrow rucked-up trousers, the curious tall hat. And once again he was standing on the edge of the platform, teetering as if about to fall on the rusty tracks.

She stopped to watch, and the late afternoon sun warmed the back of her neck. He looked very unsteady. In spite of herself and the instructions she was always given not to talk to strangers, especially men, she could not help but call out.

"Be careful," she shouted. "You'll fall."

No answer. No movement.

Alison suddenly felt that he was not alone on the platform. Indeed she thought she could see something – she was not sure what – between him and the station building. A shadow. Something was moving with paralysing slowness out of the old building towards the overbalancing man.

Alison blinked, as one who cannot believe her eyes. And in the space of the blink, both of them – the man and shadow – disappeared.

She said nothing about it at home. Her brothers would tease her; her father would not believe her; her mother would be worried that she had called to the man. Strangers should be avoided.

Even so, she had to share it with somebody. Who? What about her best friend? Sarah Coltsfoot lived opposite the old station: her parents kept a newsagent's.

Next morning, she passed the station as usual. It was bathed innocently in morning sunshine and she wondered if after all she was mistaken. Then she met Sarah Coltsfoot.

It was a mistake to confide in her. Sarah laughed. "You've got a boyfriend hidden in there," was her only remark. Alison was furious.

He was there again when she walked home. He stood on the platform's edge, looking even more likely to overbalance than ever. His face was half-turned to her but she could not make out his features, much less his age. And, as before, there was a shadow behind him, slightly nearer.

She spoke aloud to herself.

"I'm going to get Sarah to see this. Then she'll believe me."

She turned to run back to the newsagent's shop, but took one last glance at the man – to see that he was gone.

For the first time a shiver of fear ran through her body. Goose-pimples and a nasty crawling feeling at the back of her neck made her lean up against the old level-crossing gates for a moment. She did not fetch Sarah.

She said little at home that night and went to bed early, to lie awake for hours looking up at the ceiling. A turmoil of thoughts was in her mind. Who – what – had she seen? Who could she tell? Nobody, if they all reacted like Sarah.

But she had to share this with somebody because what was happening to her was very strange, quite mystifying and must be given an explanation. But who could she turn to? She mentally rejected, one by one, all her friends from school.

Then she remembered Tom Cavanagh.

Everybody, including Alison, thought Tom Cavanagh a bit of a joke. They were sorry for him as well. He was a happy, lively little soul not in the football and pop music world of the rest of them but in his own innocent world of old trains and buses. While the rest of the boys vied to see what trendy variations they could legally make on their school uniforms, Tom Cavanagh kept to his thick grey serge trousers and sensible black shoes with toecaps. While the other boys talked about United and Spurs and wondered about the girls, he saved up for long railway trips behind steam engines or visits to old bus and traction engine rallies. And he talked to no one about his great loves because nobody was interested.

But this wasn't why people felt sorry for him. He might have been laughed at had it not been for one fact

44

everybody knew. His parents were dead for many years – killed in a car crash when he was only seven. Tom had been rescued from the wrecked car quite unharmed and since then had been looked after and brought up by his elder brother, twelve years older, who regarded him with a fierce and protective love which moved everybody who saw it.

The two of them – Tom and his elder brother Ray – lived in a little terraced house near the old station directly opposite Sarah Coltsfoot's newspaper shop. Ray worked in a garage and made extra pin-money by servicing old cars for untaxed cash in the yard at the back of the house. The neighbours would have complained had anyone else done it.

Like his younger brother, Ray loved his railways; the untidy house was knee-deep in old railway posters, books, timetables, magazines, half-finished models, name-plates, "No smoking" and "Ladies Only" signs.

And because she knew him, trusted him for his wide-eyed niceness – and as her problem was connected with the railway he seemed to be the best person to approach – Alison decided to tell Tom Cavanagh all about her strange meetings and hear what he had to say.

She buttonholed him at school, during the lunch-break. She made it look as though the merest chance placed her next to him in the queue at the cafeteria. She waited until he had selected his pizza, picked up his little plastic bowl of chips, stood while a ladleful of baked beans were sloshed over his plate, taken a cream bun with a sad glacé cherry on the top, given up his dinner ticket and fished in his pocket for the extra 5p the till-lady demanded. Alison then followed him to a vacant table, carrying her own tray of corned beef salad and a dish of pale pink yoghurt. She knew full well that Tom would not seek out company in the dining hall and she felt the odd looks cast in her direction from such as Sarah Coltsfoot as she sat down opposite him.

45

It was very hard to begin talking. For a moment, Alison decided that she would say nothing after all – then once again she thought, if not Tom, then who? And she would have to be quick. Tom did not believe in hanging around. Chips and baked beans were flying into his mouth at an incredible rate: half his pizza had disappeared in one gulp. He would be gone before she started.

"Tom, listen to me," she managed to blurt out.

Tom looked up, surprised at being addressed directly.

"Yeah?" he said.

And she told him all about the strange figure at the old railway station.

By the time she had finished, the glacé cherry was entering the dark for ever and Tom was wiping the cream round his face with his fingers and licking them appreciatively. Then he spoke.

"Down at the station?"

"Yes."

"Doesn't speak?"

"No."

"Disappears when you look away and dresses old-fashioned?"

"Yes."

"Well, it's a ghost then, isn't it?"

Alison's first reaction was to get up and take her dirty plates to the hatch in disgust, even though she hadn't finished her yoghurt. First Sarah had laughed at her and now Tom, of all people, was doing the same.

Then she looked again at his round, pink face and his shining brown eyes, his short hair standing straight up as though he had had a fright in the night and his grey-brown teeth with a patch of decay right in the middle and knew instinctively that Tom Cavanagh could never laugh at anybody or say anything which was not meant completely literally. So she considered what he had said and realised – with her second stab of fear and a crawling feeling at the back of her neck – that it was what she had thought all along and yet not admitted to herself.

46

Tom continued.

"Definitely a ghost. It must be the ghost of someone who's had an accident there, like he fell off the platform and got chopped up by a train going through."

"Ugh! Horrible," said Alison.

"Happened all the time," said Tom. "Look at that chap Huskisson the day they opened the Liverpool and Manchester. Engine ran over his legs; sliced them both off. Bled to death."

If it was all to do with railways, Tom was a mine of information.

"Anyway, I can easy find out who it is," said Tom.

"How?" said Alison.

"Look it up. Got lots of books at home. *Railway Magazines.* Histories of all the pre-grouping companies. Accounts of accidents. Great disasters. All of them. Soon find out about this bloke."

This news, that Tom possessed stacks of reference information in which he was obviously thoroughly at home, surprised Alison. He showed no interest in books at school and was the English teacher's despair.

"Tell you what," said Tom. "We'll have a look at the old station. After school. Make sure nobody's got in. No use looking for a ghost if it's someone real all the time."

Alison suddenly wished she had never started this. Asking Tom was one thing; actually accompanying the weird little creature alone on some conspiratorial quest was quite another. She was just about to refuse – then knew that she couldn't. Tom was so obviously looking forward happily to it. Somebody taking notice.

"But what if the man's there?" she said.

"Then I'll see him as well," said Tom gleefully. "I've always wanted to see a ghost."

That settled it. For once Alison was not alone as she reached the level-crossing gates. They climbed over and picked their way along the weed-tangled ballast, the rotting sleepers and the rusty tracks, under the signal box with its glassless windows, till they came to the two platforms.

47

"Why haven't they knocked all this down and taken the rails away?" said Alison. "It's horrible, left to fall to bits like this."

"Ah," said Tom. "I know why. But I'm not telling. Not yet."

"Why not?"

"You'll know soon," said Tom. "But I mustn't say now."

He was suddenly shaking with suppressed excitement, as if a secret was about to burst from him. But Alison took no notice. What could daft little Tom know?

They were now on the platform, just at the point where Alison had seen the man standing. There was no sign of life at all: no trace of anybody ever having been there. Alison looked up and down the line, at familiar ~~ ntryside from a completely new angle. Everything was ~~ quiet, as if the town she knew so well was miles away.

~~ er her head was the canopy of the station roof; behind her in its shade was the booking hall from which – she remembered – that peculiar shadow had seemed to emerge. She turned round and went inside. It was very dark and smelt musty. When her eyes were used to the darkness, she made out the old ticket window and waiting room door and realised that the light was kept out by the thick boards which walled up the entrance from the road outside. So how could the man – or the shadow – have entered the station?

"Hey, come up here." A voice far off reached her. She went back to the platform. Tom was standing on the overbridge. Despite herself, Alison wanted to join him.

"Is it safe?" she said.

"Of course it is," he said. "It's great up here. Come on."

So she cautiously climbed the steps, finding them perfectly firm, and stood with Tom looking up and down the double-track line, seeing its old but to them strangely new perspectives stretching away both to the east and west.

"All right," said Tom. "Now you've climbed up here I'll tell you why all the rails haven't been torn up like they have everywhere else."

"Why?" said Alison.

"Because we're going to open the station again," said Tom triumphantly.

Alison stared at him.

"What do you mean?" she said.

"What I say," said Tom. "There's a preservation society. Ray and me, we're in it. And there's some people with a lot of money. There's one going to give us a steam engine he's got running and a couple of carriages. And there's some old lawyer bloke who got British Rail to stop pulling the rails up until it was all sorted out. Yes, we'll be running trains again along here soon."

Tom's use of "we" made it seem as though he was in charge of the whole operation. Alison decided she didn't believe him.

"I'm going home," she said.

Tom hadn't been much use. The mystery was no nearer being solved. The station was a filthy dump. Who would ever want to go on a dirty old train there? Even if one ever ran. Which she doubted.

She ran down the steps and along the track to the crossing gates and the road, leaving Tom leaning over the parapet of the bridge lost in his own little world.

Next day, she never spoke to Tom, nor he to her. She pushed the whole business right to the back of her mind.

That evening going home, she saw the man again. He was still frozen on the edge of the platform. The shadow seemed nearer. And something about the man's attitude suggested nameless and desperate fear and inconsolable sorrow.

The next few days for Alison were very unpleasant. First of all, she was teased about Tom. This infuriated her and led her to call him a silly little twit she wouldn't be seen

49

dead with. That in turn made her feel guilty: Tom might be a nuisance but she had started it. Besides this, Tom was not helping her at all. He just didn't notice how she was being teased; he followed her around bursting with things to tell her about the old railway and was plainly hurt when she ignored him at every turn. And she knew he was hurt. But she couldn't help it.

And twice more she saw the figure. Each time the suggestion of fear and sorrow was stronger. The second time Alison began to distinguish between them. The sorrow was his: the fear was hers. She was thankful when the weeks passed, July came and school ended. The holidays brought an end to the pressure.

As soon as school broke up, Alison's family went to Devon for a fortnight. It was a good holiday: Alison forgot all her worries. They all came back sunburnt, refreshed and happy.

It was another ten days before Alison saw Tom again. She was shopping: his familiar voice called after her as she came out of Boots and though she pretended she hadn't heard he soon caught up and fell into step beside her.

"You never came to see about the accident," he said.

Alison strode on without answering.

"I've got all the books and things ready. We could go through them together and find out who that man you saw is."

Alison walked on, silent and tight-lipped. Tom would not give up.

"Did you see the local paper last week? It's true what I said. We're opening the railway. We'll do up the station and clear the track. We'll run trains up the line to the next station and back."

Still no answer from Alison.

"We'll have trains on weekends and holidays. And there'll be a museum there. People will come for miles. We'll make a bomb."

Alison looked straight ahead and kept on walking.

50

"We're going to make the station like new. Why don't you come and help? I bet we'll have it ready by next Easter. It'll be marvellous. Steam's coming back."

Although she tried, Alison couldn't stop a feeling of amused affection for little Tom as he capered happily round her – and hated herself for the way she had ignored him before.

"All right," she said. "I will come round and find out who it was. I ought to clear it all up."

Alison said "was" quite automatically and was surprised at herself because of it. But a long time – nearly a month – had passed since she had seen the figure. She had a strong feeling it would not be seen again.

Alison called at Tom's house next day. She had almost convinced herself that Tom was right. If they could find an account of a nineteenth-century gentleman who had unfortunately overbalanced while a train came in and died under its wheels then the mystery would be solved. The station was haunted by the ghost of this man who had perished so terribly. But why had nobody seen him before? Alison's mind wanted to believe: she reasoned that always before the station had been too busy, too crowded for a ghost and that now it was deserted nobody ever came to see. Except her, because she was the only person who ever passed – and the first time she saw him the purest chance had made her look. He could have been there hundreds of times before without her noticing.

The front room on Tom's little house was entered straight through the door on the street. As soon as she stepped inside she noticed a lingering smell of frying bacon and soggy cabbages. She also saw magazines, books and papers all over the chairs and tables which Tom was doing his best to clear away.

"Here we are," he said, lifting a pile of back numbers of *The Railway World* off the seat of an easy chair and plonking them on the gateleg table. "Sit here."

Alison dutifully sat on the chair which emitted a curious squeaky sound as if in mild protest. Tom sat on the floor in front of her, with a little separate pile of magazines and books towards which he waved his left arm like a car salesman pointing out an incredible bargain.

"All here," he said. "Everything about our line."

Alison thought it strange that obviously quite a large amount of paper and print had been expended on the crumbling ruin across the road, but said nothing.

"First, here's what I've found out," said Tom. "Then you'll have to have a look as well."

Alison inwardly groaned.

Tom flourished a thin book with spiral binding and large thick pages.

"Pre-grouping Gazetteer," he said. "Maps of all the railways as they were built. Here's ours." And he pointed to a map of England covered in spidery lines of different colours. In the middle, creeping shortly from east to west, was a blue line crossing confident red and green lines shooting northwards.

"The East and West Midland Junction Railway. That's us. Look at the date it was built. 1865. It crossed all the big railways, like the Great Northern, the Midland and the North Western. I suppose it wasn't very big itself, though." His last words shaded off into disappointment.

"I suppose that's why it closed," said Alison, feeling a curious sympathy.

The door in the far corner of the room opened and a dark-haired man in his mid-twenties, wearing oily overalls, entered. It was Ray.

"Hallo," he said to Alison, without showing any surprise. "You'll be all right then, Tom, will you? I'm off back to the garage."

Through the door, Alison could see a tiny kitchen and she realised with a little shock that Ray must come home every day during the school holidays from the garage up the road where he worked on peoples' new Volvos to cook Tom a midday meal. And when he finally came home in the evening he spent another few hours working on a different clientele's old bangers.

She looked at him with new eyes. Poor Ray. Life must be pretty terrible for him.

"'Course I'll be all right," said Tom.

"I'll be home at six," said Ray, and left the house through the back kitchen door.

Tom took no notice, but picked up an enormous and old-looking green-bound book.

"*The Railways of the Midlands,*" he said. "That's got a whole chapter on us."

He passed the book over.

"You have a look at the chapter," he said. "I read through it, but I might have missed something. Chapter 7, it is."

Privately, Alison thought it very unlikely that Tom had missed anything. Perhaps he was deferring to someone everybody thought was good at English at school. But Alison knew she could never find her way round this lot the way Tom could. She turned to Chapter 7 (sure enough, entitled *The East and West Midland Junction Railway*) and found it started as an incredibly boring account of Acts of Parliament, share subscriptions, raising of capital and endless lists of Chairmen, Treasurers and Secretaries. She turned over the pages – and was suddenly halted by a misty, grainy photograph which, though well over a century old, was instantly familiar to her. Her own station, as seen from the level crossing gates. But how different. Plainly there were flags and bunting everywhere. An ungainly, long-funnelled steam engine stood at one platform. And there were people on the platforms: seemingly hundreds – women in long dresses, men dressed in tall hats and swallowtail coats of a sort she was now very used to.

"We're getting warm," she said.

On the platform opposite the engine stood what appeared to be a brass band. The caption said: "Scenes of joy in June 1865 as the E & WMJR is opened. Note the decorations for the occasion and the unique pre-1896 somersault signals, all removed when the Great Central railway took over the E & WMJR."

Alison wasn't interested in the pre-1896 signals, nor the decorations. But all those people. Could one of them have had a dizzy turn and fallen in front of that ancient locomotive now frozen for ever to the spot in the book?

The photograph stayed mute. She glanced down the opposite page. A paragraph caught her eye.

The Argus and Mercury for that week reported the occasion well.

"*To loud 'Huzzas' from the populace assembled on the platform and to the strains of 'See the Conquering Hero Comes' played by the Silver Band, the first train drew in, hauled by locomotive No. 1 'Bucephalus'. From the Directors' Saloon descended the Chairman of the Company, Sir Digby Cranham-Jesty, Bart; the Board of Directors; the Bishop of Towcester, the Rt Rev. Inigo Threadgold D.D. and the main contractor to the company, Mr Brassey. Sir Digby was presented with an illuminated address by the Mayor, the Worshipful Mr Burke, and the Corporation. The entire party then retired to a nearby hostelry where a cold collation was in readiness.*"

That was all. Nobody had fallen on to the rails, even after leaving the nearby hostelry.

"I can't find anything here," she said.

"There's only one more book," said Tom. "I've been through everything else." This last book had a paper cover and was typed rather than printed. Its title was *Our Local Railways: A Valediction*. The author's name was familiar: after a moment she remembered – to her surprise – that it was the solicitor her father sometimes consulted about the battery farm business. Suddenly interested, she read on. There was a page of acknowledgments – *The author acknowledges with gratitude the help and information given freely by many people, especially the following . . .* and third in the alphabetical list of twelve people was – *Mr Ray Cavanagh*.

"Ray helped with this," Alison exclaimed.

"'Course he did," said Tom. "So did I."

The longest chapter in the book was called *The Old East and West*. It told the whole story right up until British Rail finally closed the line. The last paragraph told her all she had come to find out.

So passed away the old East and West. Not the greatest railway in the land – but always, in spite of its many changes of fortune, an organisation which kept its own traditions, its own individuality. For one hundred and thirteen years it served the locality well through rain and shine, drought and flood, war and peace, never letting its people down. And in that time there was not one single fatality connected with it. That is a record the modes of transport that have succeeded the Old East and West can never boast.

Alison held the book open at this last page and poked it at Tom.

"Look," she said accusingly. "It says here, quite plainly, that no one was ever killed on the line. You must have known that. Why drag me here?"

Tom looked abashed.

"Well, yes," he said. "I know that's what the book says. I thought he might have forgotten one, though, or missed one out. You never know."

"So there's nobody," said Alison.

"We *could* have found one nobody had heard of," said Tom.

The back door suddenly opened. Ray was home.

Alison looked at her watch in amazement. It was five past six. The afternoon's reading had really absorbed her after all. So how could she be cross?

"I must be going home now, Mr Cavanagh," she said. "Goodbye, Tom."

"Oh, dear. Won't you stay and have a cup of tea?" said Ray – almost, Alison thought, wistfully.

"No, thanks," she said. Somehow she didn't fancy one there. "I must get home."

"See you when we start painting, then," said Ray. "You'll be there, won't you?"

"Painting?" said Alison.

"The old staton. All hands to the brushes. We'll make it shine."

Alison left without promising anything.

Walking over the level-crossing, she could not help but steal a glance up towards the old station. It was quite empty. She had not expected to see the overbalancing man: now she knew that he was not a ghost from the station's past she began to doubt whether she ever had. Perhaps she only imagined it. The early evening sunshine seemed to smooth out all the cracks and hide all the blemishes in the station: for a moment she saw it as in the old photograph – but now in colour, with red, white and blue bunting and a smart green engine with polished brasswork hissing on the rails; the bright colours of the ladies' dresses; the warm red of the new brickwork. And with a quickening of the heart she realised something else. Soon, it might be like that again.

Before August was out the station was descended on by hordes of volunteers. Some worked all through the week – were evidently taking their holidays there. Many more came at weekends – the concourse outside the station was full of cars and the air resounded with unfamiliar accents. Obviously people were attracted from all over the country. At first, Alison watched, fascinated. She watched groups clearing and resurfacing the platform. She watched other groups scything the banks of the trackway: yet other groups laboriously weeding between the rails. She watched bricklayers replacing crumbling bricks and repointing sound ones. She watched carpenters knocking out rotted door frames and replacing them and glaziers putting new glass in the windows. She saw Tom there every day and Ray there on Saturday afternoons and Sunday mornings. Gradually, the excitement of it all transmitted itself to her. One morning just before school started she saw Tom as he hurried down the road.

56

"Do you still want some brush-wielders?" she said.

"Yeah," said Tom. "As many as we can."

"I'll be there," said Alison.

And she was. Every Saturday found her with a huge distemper brush sloshing emulsion paint over the walls of the ticket office, the waiting room and the booking hall. She helped paint doors and window-frames; she scrubbed floors and wooden seats. The old building was beginning to look new again. By the time in October when the main work was called off until the following year, it really did seem as though Easter would see a whole railway working again.

Alison watched Tom and Ray all this time. Tom was in his element. He sandpapered, scrubbed and painted with huge effort though little accuracy and was looked on as a mascot by all the volunteers. Seeing how he was treated and comparing how he got on at school made Alison feel ashamed. Ray was different. He worked quietly, withdrawn and patient. Often he would pause in what he was doing to watch Tom protectively.

At the beginning of October, however, neither Tom nor Ray were seen much in the station. A huge articulated low-loader had arrived, bearing an old diesel shunting engine: a hired crane had placed it on the rails of a siding – and from then on Ray's job was settled. As a motor mechanic, he had to get it fit for the rails – the E & WMJR's first new motive power.

A week before the main work stopped for the winter, there was great rejoicing. There had been an inspection of the work and the track and – "The Light Railway Order's through. We've got it," yelled Tom, bouncing up and down with delight.

"The what?" said Alison.

"The Light Railway Order. We're laughing. We can run trains. No one can stop us."

And he waved the filthy black rag he had brought from cleaning the diesel shunter's insides round and round his head in ecstasy. Tom was not the only delighted person there. Everbody took time off to discuss how to open the line. Easter was already decided on – but how could they make a big day of it?

"I wonder what it was like on the first opening day?" said one person.

"I know," said Alison. "I've seen a picture."

"It's in our book," shouted Tom and had disappeared in a flash to fetch it.

When he returned, everybody crowded round to look at the picture of the opening back in 1865 and to read about it.

"I'm a photographer," said a woman in dungarees with a scarf tied round her head. "I could get this blown up and we could have it displayed in the booking hall."

"And we could follow that day as far as possible," said someone else. "Bunting, brass band, a party dressed up to look like Sir Digby Whatsit and the Bishop of Thing being welcomed by the Mayor. It would be great. I'd quite fancy a quick cold collation after it all."

"The committee would have to decide about that," said the photographer.

"They're bound to agree," said the first person. "They'd love it. So will the Mayor. We'll be bringing a lot of money into this town."

The discussion went on. It was nearly midday: Alison was going shopping with her mother in the afternoon so she left them all to it.

The days were shortening: it was soon dark every evening when Alison arrived home. The term wore on: came to an end. Christmas came and went: January, February. Half way through February work started again – the last push to have everything ready for the great re-opening by the Old East and West Preservation Society. In March there was great excitement. Once again an articulated low-loader drove up to the station: this time a steam engine was lowered on to the tracks. Not one that had

58

ever been seen on the Old East and West before – it was a little industrial saddle-tank that had spent most of its life pushing trucks round a factory siding. But it was a start. Though tiny, it was called "Hercules" – and indeed Alison thought that from the front it did look rather like "Bucephalus" in the photograph.

The weekend afterwards, the diesel engine made a trip down the line to the junction with the main line. Besides the driver, Ray was in the cab in case anything went wrong – and so was Tom. Quite obviously, this was the greatest moment so far of Tom's life. Alison watched the level-crossing gates open and the little diesel roar shakily down the track, black exhaust blurring the sky. Two hours later it returned, pulling two old carriages the Society had bought.

The week after, and "Hercules" was in steam. Echoes were raised by the sharp bark of its puffing exhaust and white steam drifted over the station, while many people in the town thought back into their childhoods when they heard the noise.

The plans for the re-opening were well advanced. It would indeed be a great occasion. The events of that June day back in 1865 would be re-enacted: the first train would arrive (actually from a siding half a kilometre up the line) and the old dignitaries – Chairman, Directors, Bishop and Contractor – would step out of it. The real Mayor would greet them and a grand celebratory lunch would be held in "The Crown". TV cameras would be there and so would local radio. It would be the biggest thing the town had seen for years. What a great way to spend Easter Monday.

The station was transformed. It was trim, neat, its signboards looking perfect. Period advertisements for Virol, Bovril and Mazawattee Tea were everywhere. The overbridge shone with new green paint. The track, weed-free and with rotting sleepers replaced by sound second-hand ones, looked dramatically different from how Alison had seen it the previous June.

Or so she thought as she walked home from school

59

three days before the Easter holidays started. She paused at the crossing and looked up the line to the station, finding it now very easy to visualize the scene in the photograph as if it were in colour.

And then she caught her breath in sudden fear.

He was there.

Just as before: the tall hat, the tail coat, the narrow trousers. About to lose his balance. Something just behind him she could not make out.

She turned away angrily. She had been so sure it had all been imagination last year: the figure had dropped out of her mind. For eight months she had been free of him: now he had returned. Why? Who was he?

She turned back. He was gone.

Next day at school, Tom sidled conspiratorially up to her.

"I know something about Easter Monday you don't know," he said.

"What's that?" said Alison. She had learnt to take Tom a lot more seriously over the last months.

"Aha!" said Tom and tapped the side of his nose with his forefinger. "You'll find out. Wait till the time comes."

Alison wanted to know.

"Oh, go on, Tom. Tell me what it is."

"I'll tell you what. You come round to our house at nine in the morning on Easter Monday. Then you'll see." He laughed delightedly. "You won't half get a surprise," he said.

Alison wondered whether to tell him her news. Then she decided against it. Tom had given all the help he could over that. So she just said, "All right. Thanks."

He was there again as she went home. How he could stay upright in the position he now showed himself – arms stretched out as if to balance, like branches on a dead tree; black-booted feet trying to cling like hands to the edge of the platform – defied explanation. And the shadow – still indescribable but something like a transparent cloud or a stained heat-haze – was almost at

60

his shoulder. As if pushing him? Alison stood dead still. Her heart hammered: the hair on the nape of her neck seemed to stand up. Yet even as she looked the apparition faded away and with it her fear. But her troubles had returned.

Next day, the station at 4.25 was innocently empty. Perhaps her visions were caused by excitement about the opening day. After all, she was far more enthusiastic about the whole thing than ever she thought she could be. And it was less than a week away.

The last day of term passed: another round of holidays started. Good Friday, Easter Saturday, Easter Day itself. Sunshine, fresh wind and fleecy clouds. Daffodils sprouted everywhere round Alison's house. Excitement was spreading through the town: Easter Monday might be a great day.

When Alison went to bed on the night of Easter Sunday she spent a long time awake thinking over all that had happened during the past year. Curious little Tom: the reclamation of a ruin and eyesore into something of life and worth: her strange hallucinations, which she realised had been directly responsible for involving her in all the rest even if they had never really happened.

But had they? She thought back over each time she had seen the apparition – if such it was. And she realised that, irregular though the intervals were, if each occasion were put together in sequence, it would be like a film in slow motion of a man falling. And the shadow. Was it, as she had thought, moving over as if to push?

No, that was silly. The whole thing was some optical illusion and she had better forget about it.

She slept. And dreamt. It was a dream of staggering, clinical clarity. Afterwards she remembered every detail so completely that it was less like a dream and more like an extra day in her life.

She was on the station platform. A warm, even wind played round everybody there and moaned through the roof canopy. The dark red bricks were new: the cement

61

between them looked hardly dry. The paving-stones of the platform were white, clean and hard-edged; red, white and blue flags and bunting were everywhere. Around her were people in Victorian clothes; women with long dresses and parasols, men with top hats and narrow trousers. On the opposite platform were hundreds of rougher, poorer-looking people, and among them stood a uniformed silver band, cornets and trombones sparkling, which she could see playing – though from them only seemed to come muted, delicate, Aeolian harmonies. All the people – the rich ones on her side of the station, the poor ones on the other, were looking up the line, to her right. As she listened, a chant of various voices started quietly and grew in volume, though the strange harmonies of the silver band remained quite clear and somehow separate. Words became audible in the chant.

"They come. They come. Sir Digby Cranham-Jesty and the Bishop of Towcester. Mr Brassey. The Board of Directors. The Bishop of Board. Sir Digby Crasty-Toaster. Mr Director. Bandy-Tasty Mr Boaster. Sir Digby Pigby Bishopy Board." And on and on, into gibberish – which merged again into a hiss of steam as everybody quietened to watch "Bucephalus" wreathed in white steam, approaching so slowly and so relentlessly with such a quiet hissing like a doll's boiling kettle.

Then Alison was aware of the man standing next to her. He was strangely familiar in his black swallowtail coat and narrow check trousers and his tall hat. She had seen him, she was sure, many times before but could not place him. And as "Bucephalus" steamed on so slowly yet so relentlessly, with no sign of stopping, the man shouted at the top of his voice, "Sir Digby. Sir Digby Cranham-Jesty", and ran towards the edge of the platform. Alison watched him, while everybody else, quite unmoved, watched the train as it steamed on. "Bucephalus" was nearly level with the man: at last, Alison managed to jerk herself into action and lunge towards him. But he had disappeared over the edge of the platform and

"Bucephalus" steamed past and squealed to a halt. Before the carriage doors opened to reveal Sir Digby Cranham-Jesty, the Board of Directors, the Bishop of Towcester and Mr Brassey, Alison had covered her eyes in horror at what had happened to the man, feeling that she was the only person there who realised or cared. As she did so she woke up on a fine Easter Monday morning.

The arrangements for Easter Monday morning were quite simple. "Hercules" would be prepared overnight. Early in the morning the volunteer driver would get steam up ready to pull the coaches to the same spot as "Bucephalus" in the old photograph. The carriages, newly painted and cleaned, were at the level-crossing side of the station: the diesel engine Ray had helped to prepare would push them through the station and half a mile past, leave them there and come back home to its little siding. Meanwhile, "Hercules" would back down the line, be coupled up to the coaches and the people representing the old Chairman, Directors and Bishop would get in and wait to be pulled decorously down the line to a flag-bedecked and crowded station and a welcome by the mayor. It would all go like clockwork: afterwards, "Hercules" would take its first fare-paying passengers down the line to the next station and would do so back and forth for the rest of the afternoon. And the Old East and West would be in business once more.

As Alison walked into town to fulfil the invitation issued by Tom, the crossing gates were shut against her. She waited, while, with a clatter, a roar and a cheery "parp" on the two-tone horn, the two maroon-painted coaches passed by, pushed by the now smart-looking green diesel.

"Hallo, love. Smashing day for it," called out the young man who was gatekeeper for the day as he opened the gates.

"It's super," said Alison and walked on. The cheerful sight of the station made her very aware of her strange dream.

Three minutes later she was at Tom's front door. The street outside was now quite busy; there was a growing trickle of people walking down to the station and cars seeking spaces in the newly re-opened car-park. For the first time ever, it had been quite difficult for her to cross the road. As she knocked at the door, there was unaccustomed noise behind her.

Tom opened it. He looked neater than she had ever seen him. He was wearing a new maroon and green jersey – a bilious-looking combination, thought Alison, but it did combine the colours of "Hercules" and its two carriages.

"All right," said Alison. "What's the big surprise?"

Tom motioned her through the door and immediately the words bubbled out of him as if his tongue could not keep up with the need to say his piece as soon as he could.

"You know they're getting a party of people to be like the ones in the photograph? Well, have you thought of who they're going to be?"

No, Alison had not even considered it. Some people would appear at the right time pretending to be their predecessors of a century before – that she realised. Who, or how, she had not bothered to think.

Tom went on with hardly a pause.

"They've chosen all the most important ones in the Society. The lawyer chap who wrote the book is going to be the bishop. And guess who's going to be Sir Digby Cranham-Jesty?"

Alison couldn't guess. Surely not Tom. It would be a needless falsification of history to portray Sir Digby as a midget.

"Well, I'll tell you who," cried Tom, his face bright red with excitement. "It's Ray. Ray's going to be the chairman."

Yes, that's nice of them, thought Alison. Quiet, patient, hard-working Ray. A little moment of glory he deserved.

"Oh, I am glad," she said. "That's lovely."

The noise of the cars moving on their way to the station

64

car-park was now loud through the window. The morning sun shone in on the same magazines, posters and books that were there the last time she was in the room.

She waited for Tom to say more. But another noise sounded; a door closing upstairs and then footsteps down a staircase.

"He's changed into his clothes. He's coming down the stairs." Tom's voice grew louder and faster. "He's here."

And in walked Ray. He was wearing a high winged collar, a brown waistcoat, a black jacket with long tails and narrow brown check trousers. His boots were shiny and black. On his face was a shy smile and in his hand was a tall hat which, as he came to the middle of the room, he placed on his head. In that enclosed space with a low ceiling he looked like a giant.

Tom shouted out in ringing tones, as if he was MC at a boxing match, "Sir Digby Cranham-Jesty."

But Alison's heart was hammering and her head swam. For a second the room seemed to go round and round; the figure with the tall hat swayed to and fro like a tree that might break in the wind. For Sir Digby Cranham-Jesty, Ray might well be.

He was also the overbalancing man who had haunted Alison for nearly a year.

"What's up?" said Ray.

Alison just stared. There could be do doubt. He was the man. But how could one version of Ray be servicing Volvos just when another was teetering on the platform in Victorian costume? What did it *mean*?

"Come on, come on, come on," shouted Tom. His excitement was out of control. "We've got to get going."

"Calm down, Tom," said Ray. "Can't you see Alison doesn't feel well? And besides, they're picking me up in the car. And you, if you want them to. You can ride on the train as well. You won't miss anything."

Tom's voice was almost feverish. "I'm on my way now. I can't wait for you lot. I'll see you at the train. I'll be there before you."

And he dashed out of the house.

Ray raised his head slightly and lowered it again, clicking his tongue as he did so.

"Typical," he said. "He can't sit still a minute."

"I'd better be off," said Alison, who still felt shaken and wanted somewhere to think.

Outside on the road there was a sudden, violent scream of brakes. The sound of car engines died away. There was silence except for running footsteps and urgent voices; Ray and Alison looked at each other – then they ran out of the house.

Thirty metres down the road towards the station a knot of people gathered round something lying in the road in front of a blue Austin Ambassador. The driver's door was open. A man sat rigid in the driver's seat. As Alison and Ray reached the crowd, a plump woman in her fifties turned to them.

"The poor driver had no chance," she said. "The boy was running hell-for-leather along the pavement and then went straight across the road, right in front of him. He stood on his brakes but it was too late."

Sirens wailed in the distance. The police and an ambulance were on their way. Alison pushed her way through the crowd with an awful feeling of inevitability. Ray followed. Together they looked down at the sprawled figure in the road.

It was Tom. Quite obviously, he was dead.

Fearfully, Alison looked at Ray – a bizarre figure in his Victorian costume with its tall hat. His face was chalk-white; his mouth slightly open; his body absolutely rigid. At the back of Alison's mind was a feeling that Ray would bend down to his dead brother, pick him up, cradle him, make some futile attempt to breathe life back into him.

But he did no such thing. He just stood there.

And then came a sound which for the last moments they had all forgotten about – a cheerful two-tone blast on the hooter of the diesel shunter, on its way back from marshalling the coaches.

Ray heard it. At once, he sprang into life. Pushing people away from him he broke into a striding run towards the station.

"I'm going with him," he shouted.

Then Alison knew what was in Ray's mind. For five years, Tom had been everything Ray had to live for. And if he was gone? Alison saw again in her mind all the times she had seen the overbalancing man; had sensed desperate sorrow. And she knew that she had seen a ghost of the future, not the past; that a moment of overpowering feeling had burst its bonds of time to call directly to her. She remembered too the shadow behind the overbalancing man which seemed to be pushing him over.

She set off in pursuit. As in a dream, her steps were leaden. She recalled how she had not been able to save the man in her dream of the night before. The memory was like a knife at her heart.

Ray kept running. He dodged between cars queuing to park. Surprised occupants stared out at him; they seemed to think it was all part of the day's events. Into the station he dashed.

All this time, the clattering roar of the diesel shunter drew nearer. As Ray staggered blindly into the booking hall it was at the end of the platform. The driver gave another chirrup on the horn. Alison was still behind Ray; gaining on him, let alone catching him, seemed impossible. As he emerged on to the platform, the shunter, travelling at a steady twelve miles an hour, was nearly under the station roof. Alison could see that when Ray reached the platform edge, the shunter would be level with him. And in her mind she saw again the overbalancing man and the shadow behind ready to push him to his death.

The roar was close, the stink of diesel exhaust was strong. The square bulk of the engine shut out the light under the station roof. Ray reached the edge. He staggered, threw up his arms so that he looked more than ever like a toppling dead tree. The engine was three metres away; the driver had applied the brakes and let out a blaring howl on the horn. But Ray would fall in its path and nothing would stop it happening.

So thought Alison as the sight unfolded in front of her. She watched helpless, as she had in the dream.

But she was not helpless. Suddenly she felt strength she never knew she had, as if from a force beyond her. She hurled herself at Ray, grabbed his right arm between shoulder and elbow, pulled downwards with all her might. Above, the dark green side of the diesel engine loomed like a cliff – a precipice down which she and Ray were falling. The gruff, tumultuous chatter of the diesel engine filled her eardrums.

Still she pulled on Ray's arm; it was like trying to hold down the sail of a clipper ship in a storm. She felt as if she would be sucked into the whirlpool of noise, darkness and machinery. Dimly, she saw two terrified faces staring down at her from the cab. Then the sun's light forced itself into her eyes as if it had emerged from a total eclipse.

The diesel shunter had passed. The whole struggle had taken three seconds. But to Alison it seemed an age. The first part of her life had led up to the moment she emerged behind Ray on the platform; the second had consisted of the time it took for the engine to go by.

Ray weakened, crumpled. Others came forward, led the two of them gently away from the platform's edge. The shunter had stopped twenty metres off; its engine ticked over quietly. The driver hurried to join the rest.

"I thought we'd killed you both," he muttered and prised Alison's fingers away from Ray's arm. The two were led into the waiting room where they sat down. Ray, his hat incredibly still in place, stared straight ahead. Together they could make no sound.

Someone brought them cups of tea; they drank as in a trance.

Then, quietly at first, but relaxing into great racking sobs, Ray began to cry. Hearing him, Alison could do the same.

* * *

68

Yes, the Old East and West was re-opened that day. But everything was muted. The re-enactment of the original opening was cancelled. As "Hercules" trundled busily up and down the line, the passengers crowding the carriages were quiet and serious.

Yet nobody suggested cancelling the re-opening. They had known Tom too well for that.

The day passed. So did succeeding days, weeks, months. Alison felt a personal grief which lay at the back of her mind whatever she was doing. And for some time, Ray lived like a hermit, no matter what many people did to try to snap him out of his sorrow.

In time, though, he recovered and appeared to forget his grief. He was even rumoured to be courting! – a motherly girl from the other side of the town. But Alison knew that a great part of him had died with Tom, even though she had managed to stop all of him from dying.

The Old East and West flourished. After a year, by popular request and – now his grief had subsided, with every acquiescence from Ray – there was a naming ceremony at the station. The diesel shunter now sported its own nameplates; it was called, simply, "Tom".

To think of what Tom's pleasure would have been at having an engine named after him brought a lump to Alison's throat.

That ceremony took place the following Easter. When it was over, Alison walked on her own back down the quiet road to her house among the trees, to her secure family, her animals and battery hens. She was thinking – more carefully than she had managed for a long time – about those last months of Tom's life; the only months she had known him. How strangely she had become entwined with his fate; solely through the ghost from the future, the overbalancing man who had warned of Tom's death.

And the shadow that had followed it. For the first time she could contemplate these memories. What had it been? Perhaps it was her own fear.

But also, it was her own resolve. For after all there was

no shadow following Ray to push him over the edge. Indeed, there was a real person of flesh and blood who had brought him back from the brink.

No wonder, then, that on those summer evenings, she could not make out the shadow's form.

She had been watching the ghost of herself.

There was a cheerful "Toot" on the line behind her. She turned round and saw, shiny in green paint with the new polished nameplate glistening in the evening sun, "Tom" clattering busily down the line, its exhaust staining purple the clear evening air.

She stayed looking until both sight and sound had disappeared. Then she walked on towards her own home.

Faces

A retelling

This retelling places in present-day Britain one of the many traditional stories from the Malay Peninsula about the obstreperous local ghost called *The Pontianak*.

The road was straight. The night was cold. The sky was clear. The moon shone pale. The tall trees by the side of the road cast narrow shadows across it, so that the man who ran, panting and frightened, had the strange impression that he was toiling up a long flight of stairs.

His heartbeats sounded like muffled drums in his ears, not quite in rhythm with his echoing feet. Sweat poured into his eyes, though the night was bitterly cold.

From time to time, a car would pass him going the other way. Its headlights would search him out and then ignore him: the lowering in pitch of the engine noise as it swept past him sounded like a contemptuous dismissal. Every now and then, without pausing in his stride, the man would steal a look behind him, half fearfully, half hopefully. And all the while, the desperation and sick dread mounted in his mind.

How long had he been running? It seemed as though he had been pounding breathlessly on, one foot in front of the other, since the moment he was born. Yet could he have run much more than a mile? And how many miles more did he have still to run?

He snatched another look behind him. Far down the road he saw what looked like two pale eyes. He turned round – though he kept running, so he was now actually

71

stumbling backwards. The eyes drew nearer. They were the headlights of a car – but not with the piercing brightness of halogen bulbs on main beam. The car drew nearer. Suddenly almost crazed with relief, the man stepped into its path, waving his arms and hardly caring for his safety. The car drew to a halt: the lights close to made the man blink.

He walked to the passenger door and the driver leant across to open it for him. The car was old: a magnificent black Daimler of pre-war vintage. For the moment, the man cared nothing for this. It was a car, and a car meant speed and escape.

"For God's sake take me to the next town," he gasped.

The driver sat back, calm and almost statuesque, in his capacious leather-upholstered seat. In the moonlight the man could see he wore a very expensive overcoat, a hat pulled low over his head and a woollen scarf. His face was in darkness, but from the depths of the scarf came a level, smooth, mellifluous voice.

"Certainly," he said.

The panting man climbed over the running board and into the car. He settled into the front passenger seat and began to breathe more easily. For some minutes the journey proceeded quietly. The muffled figure behind the wheel drove speedily along the straight, dark road. The old but perfect car hummed regally along. Its new passenger regained his breath completely and with it some of his composure.

At length the driver spoke. The first impression of calm evenness in his voice was confirmed.

"Tell me, sir – for indeed I could not help but notice the state you were in when I stopped for you – the cause of your perturbation."

The passenger gulped. For a moment it seemed as though he was unwilling to say anything at all about his experiences. Then – in the warm, steadily-driven car, insulated from the evils of the dark night outside, he relaxed.

"Very well," he said.

And then he commenced his story.

"My own car," he said, "broke down about three miles back along the road. The useless thing was completely dead: I tinkered around with what tools I had but it was hopeless. I needed help. I realised I was miles from anywhere on a lonely road I had never seen before. What could I do? I just had to lock the car up and walk. Perhaps, I reasoned, there might be a house nearby where perhaps I could get help – or at least make a telephone call.

"I must have walked for well over a mile without seeing any sign of life. I almost decided to go back and sleep in the car till morning. How I wish I had."

He paused for a moment.

"Go on," the driver said.

"Then I saw a house standing back from the road. The wrought-iron gates were open: a weedy, gravelled drive led up to a dark front door. It was a large house with a high-pitched roof and leaded windows with small panes. There were no lights on: it seemed deserted. But the front gate was open, so perhaps it was worth calling. Somebody might be there to help me. So I scrunched up the gravel drive to the front door, saw a bell-pull and, naturally enough, pulled it.

"Almost before the bell started jangling through the house, the front door opened. The surprise of that – almost as if whoever was behind the door had been waiting for the bell to ring – took my breath away.

"In the doorway stood a figure. I had a definite impression that it was a woman, though she was carefully shading the candle she held so that nothing of her was revealed but only the bare floorboards and walls of the entrance hall in which she stood.

"'Come inside,' she said.

"Her voice was low and resonant in the empty hall. She turned away from me, beckoning as she did so. Without questioning my action at all, I followed her. She led me up

73

uncarpeted stairs and paused on the landing. The candle was still the only source of light.

"In the shadows, I could make out several closed doors. But one door – I could tell by a very faint bar of light stretching vertically from lintel to floor – was open. A voice called out from behind it. It was a man's voice – and it too had a clarity and sweetness of tone that rings in my ears even now.

"'Who is it, my dear?'

"The woman answered with words that should have chilled my heart.

"'It is he whom we have expected.'

"Yes, I know I should have turned tail and run away then – away from that accursed place for ever. But I did not. For the feeling still uppermost in me was relief at having found help and shelter with people who sounded so kind.

"The woman led me to the open door. I saw then where the light had come from. The moon was now fully up and its cold light poured in through the curtainless, leaded windows opposite me. Between me and the window was a large table with what looked to be an oil-lamp placed on it. And behind the table was the shape of a man, standing.

"The woman moved away from me to stand beside him.

"For a moment, there was complete silence and stillness. I waited for something to happen, something more to be said.

"Then the man leant forward. There was a scratch, a sudden flare from a match. He had lit the lamp. A warm, yellow light threw shadows round the room. I blinked in sudden surprise: I had become used to semi-darkness. So I looked round at this bare room, at the beams of the ceiling, the great oak table, the heavy, carved chairs pushed back against the walls. And I looked at my new companions, now that I had light to see them with.

"And then my face froze into horror and my voice formed itself into a wordless scream.

"For the faces of both the man and the woman were the

same. No mouth. No nose. No eyes. They were smooth, bare, featureless – as eggs."

Here the storyteller paused and shuddered, as if the memory was too much for him. The driver said nothing – the Daimler purred on its way. The storyteller took a deep breath and continued.

"Without thinking twice, I turned and ran. I swept through the doorway, almost fell down the stairs in my headlong rush, fought desperately to push the front door open till I remembered it opened inward, stumbled along the gravel drive and out again on to the road. I listened for footsteps behind me: I heard none. I took one last look at the house as I passed the open gates: at the lighted window of that upstairs room I could see the two human-seeming silhouettes surveying my departure.

"On I ran, the way I had been going before, desperate for help, for consolation, for assurance that I had been merely the victim of a mistake, a practical joke, a hallucination, perhaps a nightmare. And then, as if in answer to a prayer, you stop for me, and I am back in the world of normality."

He gave a sigh of relief and satisfaction and settled comfortably and confidently back in the soft leather seat as the Daimler sped smoothly onward.

The driver's hands stayed calmly on the steering wheel. For almost the first time since the passenger had commenced his story, he spoke.

"You say their faces had no features on them. Were they, in fact, quite blank?"

"Yes," said the passenger.

The driver turned to his companion and with his left hand removed his scarf.

"You mean," he said, "like this?"

No mouth. No nose. No eyes. A face as blank and smooth and featureless as an egg.

His Last Lesson:
Sharon Kane's Testimony

I suppose the weirdest thing that ever happened to me was when I was still at school.

It was the very last day of the summer term – the last full lesson of the year. History. And that old idiot Pearson was taking us. For his last lesson.

My name, by the way, is Sharon Kane. I've left school now: I've got a job in Sainsbury's. All this was three years ago. But I still wake up in the middle of the night remembering it.

That July day marked the end of my fourth year at the Theodore Hungerford Comprehensive. It marked a few other things as well, as it turned out.

There's no doubt about it, old Pearson looked really out of place with us lot. He must have been over sixty: he'd taught in the old Grammar School before they moved the Job Centre and the Marriage Guidance people into the buildings and merged the school with two others to make the TH Concentration Camp. The poor old twerp never got over it. Half his friends from the old school emigrated rather than teach at TH. Perhaps they thought they'd be lined up and shot if they didn't. Old Pearson had stuck it for eight years. But enough was enough for him, I suppose, and now he was retiring. All that time teaching and it was due to fizzle out with us – fourth year History bottom set, CSE if we were lucky. This is what he'd come to. How are the mighty fallen. He must have wanted to weep when he remembered the clever devils who used to hang on every word he said.

He was tall and thin, was old Pearson: bald on top with wispy grey hair over his ears. He had one of those quick, stammery, posh voices teachers never seem to have nowadays. It's a pity there's not more of them because he was very easy to imitate. It made him go berserk with fury. That's why, of course, Kevin Benwell was going to record his last lesson. When old Pearson's voice disappeared from TH school a light would go out of our lives. We had to have something to remember him by. Poor old fool. He must have hated us.

Anyway, he gave us something to remember him by all right.

It was a lovely sunny afternoon. Outside the window you could see the bike sheds, part of the staff car park and the music and drama block, far away from the rest of the school so they could only deafen each other. Beyond that was the council estate most of us lived on. It stretched for miles until it lost itself in the industrial estate where most of our parents worked. Though as there was a bit less industry every year, there were fewer of our parents there every year as well. They'd never got inside the Grammar School building when they were kids but they did now the Job Centre was in it. And some of them ended up in the Marriage Guidance.

What a dump.

Anyway, Kevin had hidden the microphone with some maths text books on the table at the front. We knew that would be all right – old Pearson was hardly your modern active teacher. He'd stay sitting rigid behind the desk and dictate the notes he'd dictated every year since he started at the Grammar School and then wonder why his CSE pupils only got grades four and five.

Kevin sat at the front (the desks were in rows in Pearson's room) with his cassette recorder on his knee. "This had better be worth it," he said before Pearson came in. "I'm using a new C 90 on him."

The door opened and in Pearson walked, a faraway, lost look in his eyes as if he was remembering the old Grammar School days when everyone stood up at the sight of him. Or so we were told. This time, though, there was a bit more quiet than usual. After all, Kevin's recorder was only a little battery thing and we wanted to pick Pearson's voice out properly. So he sat at his table amid surprising quiet. And then he turned and looked at us and said nothing.

Something about his face made us really silent. I don't know about the others, but it suddenly dawned on me that this was a big day in his life. This was the end. After today he'd never teach again. Forty-odd years, a hundred and twenty-odd terms, something like sixty thousand-odd lessons. And this was the last.

What he said then made me see that he was thinking the same. But it seemed a bit odd to say it to us. Especially in that quick, posh, stammery voice.

"I always wanted to teach, you know. And nothing was going to s-stop me. N-nothing."

"Not even us?" muttered Shaun Crystal at the back but someone said, "Sssh" and Shaun shut up and so did everybody else. Somehow we were all looking at old Pearson.

"S-something rather odd happened, you know, when I was a s-student," he went on. "As this is my v-very last lesson, I might as well t-tell you."

Nobody said a word, but I could see Kevin Benwell's eyes were on the VU meter to watch the recording level.

"When I was at University, you know, there was a m-murder. Someone I knew v-very well. They hanged people for murder in those days. The p-person who was hanged was someone else I knew very well."

Honestly, you'd have thought we'd all been turned to stone. Kevin was still staring at his meter but I could see his eyes were popping out of his head. I bet in all his forty years teaching Mr Pearson had never had quieter class — one that wasn't taking notes, that is.

"Sh-shall I go on?" old Pearson said.

Nobody moved except Tracey Purvis who nodded her head up and down as if it would fall off.

"I went to University at Abbasridge," he went on. "I don't suppose you've heard of it. It's the very oldest University in Britain. Far older than Oxford or Cambridge. And it's very tiny. Who knows where Abbasridge is?"

Nobody answered, partly because nobody knew and partly because it was only the second proper question he'd asked us all the time we'd known him and the first was only ten seconds before. But like most teachers he was going to tell us the answer anyway.

"Abbasridge is a cathedral city, in the west country, close to the Mendip Hills. An ancient place, with Arthurian connections, a magnificent cathedral with the tallest spire in the country and three old, worn grey limestone courtyards which formed the colleges of the University. It was the best place to study history because history was all round you. King Arthur came there and King Alfred came there and after them came every King and Queen, Lord and Bishop of note in the land – at some time or other in their lives, for there in Abbasridge lay the country's soul."

He took his glasses off to wipe them and you could see that he wasn't with us any more – he was miles away, far from rotten old TH in place and time so we had to wait for him to come back.

"It was a rare privilege to be there, you know. To be breathing the air so many great men had breathed before me. A rare privilege for a poor boy from a poor home like myself."

That surprised us. You'd have thought he was born with his posh accent and that his mother had mixed chalk-dust with his Farley's Rusks.

"It was that place which resolved me to teach," he said. "I wanted to pass on this great heritage to you and people like you."

I suppose he couldn't help but look out of the window at the vandalised phoneboxes and the spray-paint on the walls. Some heritage.

"The little town of Abbasridge," he said. "The narrow streets crowding, curling round the hill: on its summit the great cathedral with its spire. Seen for miles around and also there facing you at every twist, every turn of those bustling, jostling streets. Always you were aware of it. It was, I suppose, a benevolent guardian. Yet sometimes it frightened me.

"In my first year at Abbasridge University I lived in lodgings at the edge of the town. Mrs Cole was the landlady. There were three of us young gentlemen, as she liked to call us. Belstrode, Wetton and myself. I must say something about Belstrode and Wetton because they loom large in my story."

Here he paused. And then he repeated, dreamily: "Yes, I must say something about Belstrode and Wetton. It is so many, many years since I said something about Belstrode and Wetton."

Another pause. And then his voice was louder, firmer.

"I watched your faces when I told you I was a poor boy. I know you all. You did not believe me. But I was. Poorer than you will ever be. But how I worked to escape that poverty. How hard I had to work. And what I missed in the doing of it."

Old Pearson saying this to us? What was happening to the world?

"A poor boy from a country school, coming into the great world with no money and only his wits to live on. Wits which were puny compared with others there. My brightness at school was dim at Abbasridge. And in my lodgings were Belstrode and Wetton. That was a cruel stroke."

I couldn't help noticing that old Pearson had lost his stammer. And his voice wasn't sounding nearly so posh as usual, either.

"Now," went on Pearson, "I want you to see very clearly what sort of people Belstrode and Wetton were. It's very important that you understand."

Yes, suddenly it did seem important.

80

"Belstrode," said Pearson. "Rich. A great bear of a man. More often than not, drunk."

We still looked at him, fascinated.

"Wetton," he said, "A genius. The best brain I have ever known. It should have been mine." He paused. "Both of them looking down on me from a great height. Belstrode – son of a banker, nephew of a Cabinet Minister – when enjoying the combination of alcohol and anger was a fearsome sight. It frightened me at such times so I kept out of his way. And it frightened people with supposedly stronger stomachs than mine. And how he tried to rile the silent, superior Wetton. Who took no notice; probably hardly knew Belstrode was there.

"Well, three terms went by; three terms which showed me what a small fish I was in the great pond of Abbasridge University. And I was lodged with two of the biggest. A barracuda and a swordfish.

"How unfair that this should happen to me. I had worked so hard to get to Abbasridge. It meant so much to me. And here were these two blighting my life, making me feel like trash. Their mocking faces followed me by day and drifted through my dreams at night."

It's funny how I remember every word of this. Old Pearson's voice seemed to have swelled out into something rich and strange which filled every corner of the room. He was picking words out of the air – that's the only way I can describe it – and stringing them together in a stream which wasn't going to stop until *he* decided when.

"My only real friend in Abbasridge was not part of the University. Mrs Cole's lodging house was, as I have said, on the very outskirts of the city – virtually, in fact, in the village of Colgurney. And it was the vicar of this tiny place who had befriended me. Like me, he was interested in history; his interest, just as I was beginning to find mine way, lay in odd objects, the little byways of fact and fancy, the tiny concerns of ordinary people, far removed from the vast and weighty matters dealt with by Wetton and his

81

like. The Reverend Mr Hopwood was an old man – a wrinkled gnome in his rambling, shabby vicarage. He was a collector: antiques, curios, books – perhaps more of a jackdaw than a collector. He was hardly systematic: the only times in those days at Abbasridge when I could truly forget myself and feel something like content was when I sat in the Vicarage attempting to bring order out of chaos – to codify his objects, to catalogue his books. Perhaps I had some notion that when he died the old man would leave this assortment to me. Vain hope: he died without a will some years after these events and relations threw away what they could not sell.

"We come at last to the central events of my story. Listen well. I shall never repeat them."

Pearson paused and fixed us with his eyes. We stared back.

"Picture an evening in early autumn. An evening of mauve light which tells you the year is dying. Through the window of Mrs Cole's dining room I could see the sun's decline in the west, settling down below the dark line of the Mendip Hills etched on the horizon. I remember looking at this view and thinking how its nostalgic melancholy echoed all my old, dashed hopes. Miles away I was, so I hardly heard Mrs Cole talking to me until she had to repeat herself.

"'I said, Where will you three gentlemen be tonight?'

"Poor Mrs Cole. The world of 'young gentlemen' to her was whole, entire and separate. She could conceive of no possible division within it. To her, the three of us must be the greatest friends.

"'I shall be at Mr Hopwood's,' I said.

"Belstrode and Wetton were not in the house; I was eating alone. Wetton, I knew, would arrive soon from his day of solitary study at the library and would be writing in his room until the small hours, with his damnable powers of complete concentration. And Belstrode?

"'Mr Belstrode,' I said, 'has a very important engagement tonight. A supper in College to celebrate some sporting triumph in which he thinks he has shared.'

"I had no need to tell Mrs Cole that Belstrode could therefore not be expected back much before three o'clock in the morning and that when he did arrive by taxi he would stagger to his bed and stay there till midday in a complete drunken stupor and that for some hours after it would not be wise to go near him. She knew Belstrode's habits. She knew what to expect.

"Nor did I think it necessary to tell her that I would stay late at Mr Hopwood's – indeed, might even consider staying the night. For I was deeply involved in the listing of a job lot of books he had picked up at a sale – in those days such things could be had for a song – and was finding more interest in the task than I had ever bargained for.

"In the event, I did not return to the house to go to bed until three o'clock in the morning. When I arrived at the Vicarage, the old man was waiting for me. 'David,' he said. 'There is something very interesting among my latest purchases. A first edition of Robert Louis Stevenson's *Weir of Hermiston*.' I could hardly share his enthusiasm for a work not fifty years old. But then, Stevenson died before he finished it, and the fascination of what might have been resolved me to read it during the long night hours. So I took the small, dark volume from Mr Hopwood and slipped it in my overcoat pocket before taking it off.

"'A pity it isn't a signed copy,' I said. The remark was wasted.

"And then I set to work, examining each new acquisition, working out a place for it in relation to the rest of the old man's sprawling, musty library. I was absorbed in what I was doing, while the old man fussed round me, brought me cups of tea and glasses of brown, sweet sherry (which I refused) and finally stretched out in a shabby easy chair and dropped into a fitful sleep with his mouth hanging open and breathy, snorting snores coming from it.

"At eleven o'clock, I went to the telephone. I asked a tired operator to connect me with Mrs Cole's Abbasridge number. Mrs Cole did not sound surprised when I told her not to wait up for me. I had a key and would let myself in during the small hours. Mrs Cole was free to retire to her room with a book, a cup of cocoa and (a secret she tried in vain to keep from us) a half-bottle of gin. Now, not even the Day of Judgment would wake her. I asked her whether Wetton and Belstrode were home.

"'Mr Wetton is working in his room,' she said. 'Mr Belstrode is still out at his party.'

"'I think you can leave Mr Belstrode to let himself in,' I said. 'He has a key of his own.'

"It always seemed strange to me that, as 'young gentlemen', we seemed able to tell Mrs Cole what she should do in her own house.

"'If you're quite sure, then, Mr Pearson,' she said. And I knew that was that.

"So it was three o'clock in the morning when I finally let myself in to my lodgings. I could see the light on in Wetton's room: it was not unusual for him to work through the night. And that Belstrode was home was perfectly obvious. As I went up the stairs I could see his door open and his light on – and him sprawled fully clothed on his bed, snoring drunkenly.

"I smiled bitterly to myself at what seemed the typicality of my colleagues' behaviour. Then I entered my own room and slept soundly until the morning.

"Mrs Cole did not seem surprised when Belstrode did not appear for breakfast. Neither was I. But she did become a little agitated about Wetton, who seemed quite capable of living without sleep, was punctual by nature, and though he consumed only the most frugal of meals, certainly never missed them.

"'Do you think I should see if he is all right?' she said to me.

"'I am sure Mr Wetton can look after himself perfectly well,' I murmured.

"'I'll take him a nice cup of tea,' said Mrs Cole. 'That will wake him up, I know.'

"The scream which Mrs Cole emitted three minutes later would have curdled the blood even of one as strong as Belstrode were he not still in his unconscious stupor. At the sound if it, I ran upstairs as fast as I could.

"And there I saw the sight Mrs Cole had screamed at. For Wetton sat slumped over his desk, the white scarf which had strangled him still round his neck. That ice-cold brain, that brilliant intellect, so much dead meat."

Old Pearson stopped here and looked out of the window. Our eyes followed his, as if we expected to see this Wetton person's dead face looking back through the glass at us. We didn't see it. But perhaps old Pearson did. You never know.

Anyway, after a few seconds, he went on.

"Mrs Cole was sitting on Wetton's unslept-in bed, pale as chalk, her mouth silently opening and shutting. I made her drink the tea she had brought for her ex-lodger, then rang the police. Having called them to the house, I tried to rouse Belstrode.

"This was difficult. The discovery of Wetton's body had been made to the background of Belstrode's stertorous breathing; he was still where I had seen him at three in the morning and still deeply unconscious. The room stank of stale alcohol. When my repeated shakings at last had their effect and his sunken eyes opened, he swore loudly at me and it was some minutes before my news that Wetton had been strangled sank in.

"'Little runt,' he said. 'No more than he deserved.'

"Then he closed his eyes again.

"'Stay awake, Belstrode,' I urged. 'The police will want to talk to you.'

"'Wake me up when they arrive,' he said, and closed his eyes again.

"Very soon they did arrive. A line of black Austins and Rovers drew up in the narrow street: the house was full of uniformed policemen and shabby, seedy-looking individuals who could only be detectives; the scene was laughably like the black-and-white crime films often shown in the nearby cinema which we 'young gentlemen' sometimes attended and poked noisy fun at to annoy the local audience.

"A small, sallow-faced man with large ears, black shiny hair plastered flat on his head and parted in the centre, wearing a light fawn belted mackintosh, detached himself from the scrum. He introduced himself as the Chief Inspector in charge of the case and intimated that Mrs Cole, Belstrode and I should accompany him back to the police station.

"A policeman was needed to cow Belstrode into submission, so that he would sober up, dress and come with us. Mrs Cole evidently needed more than Wetton's cup of tea: she had lapsed into noisy hysterics, from which she was released only by some swigs from her nearly empty gin bottle. She had now quietened down to monotonous repetition of 'In my house? What, in my house?' which reminded me uncomfortably of Lady Macbeth.

"So the three of us were bundled into the back seat of a large police Austin 18 and whisked through the narrow, twisting streets, under the disapproving stare of the cathedral spire, to the new, cold, functional, concrete police station on the other side of the city. And there the three of us waited, in separate rooms, for the Chief Inspector to question us.

"Mrs Cole was the first to go in. What transpired between the two I never knew. When my turn came I found the Inspector was most anxious about my movements on the previous night.

"Could I prove that I was where I said I was? Well, of course, the Vicar of Colgurney (no less) would vouch for me. What was I doing at the Vicarage? Well, of course, I was cataloguing his new books? Could I prove it? Providentially, at that moment, I plunged my hand into my overcoat pocket and found *Weir of Hermiston*.

"'See, Inspector,' I said. 'One of his books. A first edition. Not rare, but interesting all the same.'

"His eyes narrowed as he looked at me.

"'No, Inspector, I did not steal it. He lent it to me to read.'

"A place was marked by a turned-down page corner. The Inspector motioned that I should hand the book over. He took it and opened it at the marked page.

"'Page 53,' he said, and started to read. '*On the named morning he was at the place of execution.*' He had turned the page and scanned the words for a second or two, before reading again. '*Then followed the brutal instant of extinction, and the paltry dangling of the remains like a broken jumping-jack.*' He paused. 'This is the sort of book you like, sir?' he said.

"'Chapter three,' I replied. '*In the matter of the hanging of Duncan Jopp*. I read it as a fine book. No more.'

"He gave me a long look and handed *Weir of Hermiston* back to me.

"'I hope you enjoy finishing it, sir,' he said.

"'I shall never finish it,' I replied. 'Poor Stevenson died not half way through the writing of it.'

"There was a very long silence indeed, while the Chief Inspector sat back in his chair and regarded me and I looked back at him with what was (I pride myself) a cool gaze. At last be broke the silence.

"'Your landlady says you rang her at 11pm saying where you were.'

"'That is correct.'

"'At 2.45. It is no more than fifteen minutes' walk.'

"'Who can vouch for this?'

"'The Vicar. Mr Hopwood.'

"'And all that time you were, er, cataloguing?'

"'I was.'

"'There must be a great many books.'

"'There are.'

"Then he changed the subject abruptly.

"'You and Mr Belstrode are hardly the best of friends, I believe.'

"'Whatever makes you think that?' I replied.

"'We can read between the lines, sir, as well as the next man,' he said. 'Now, how would you feel about enraging Mr Belstrode when he was under the influence of drink?'

"'I can assure you, Inspector,' I said, 'that I think too much of my personal safety to do any such thing.' And I laughed as I said it.

"It was meant to sound as a humorous remark. But the Chief Inspector did not seem to take it humorously. He looked morosely at me.

"'Mr Belstrode is a violent man, then?'

"'He can be at times.'

"'Had Mr Wetton crossed him?'

"'Inspector, surely . . . no, I am not aware of his having done so.'

"The interview soon ended. A statement was written out; I read it and signed.

"Soon, Mrs Cole and I were back in the house, with requests to be available if required. Belstrode did not come back with us.

"Next day, Belstrode was charged with Wetton's murder."

Outside the classroom the sun had gone in; clouds were forming over Theodore Hungerford. Most of us in the room shivered. But old Pearson didn't. He was miles away.

"The strength of the case against Belstrode lay in three main points. First – the white scarf used to strangle Wetton belonged to him. He was quite unable to deny this. Second – the outside knob of Wetton's door was covered in Belstrode's fingerprints while that inside was not. The police therefore inferred that he had opened the door, murdered Wetton with it left open and closed it behind him. The third was his well-known violent temper which could lead – when the drink was on him – to murderous rages. Belstrode's defending counsel – I know

88

this for a fact – tried to make him plead guilty to manslaughter only, saying that he was drunk and had no recollection of the killing. Belstrode refused this and persisted in asserting his complete innocence. Which meant that, having to establish his complete innocence, the defending counsel had to try to implicate me or Mrs Cole. There was no point in thinking about an unknown intruder: the police were certain there was none. So, if not Belstrode, who?

"The trial came: the little wooden-raftered court-room at the Abbasridge Assizes was packed. A murder trial involving a young gentleman of the University: that was something worth turning out for.

"I was, of course, cross-examined – the same sorts of question as the Chief Inspector asked. Could Mr Hopwood vouch for my being in the Vicarage all the time I said I was? He could: He will. How could I be sure that I had phoned Mrs Cole when I said I had? Surely incontrovertible proof would come from the manual telephone exchange – the operator would undoubtedly have logged the call. Could I prove that I had left the Vicarage at 2.45? Of course I could: the evidence of a gentleman of the cloth is surely unimpeachable. And so, of course, it proved. Dear old Mr Hopwood was adamant that he, yes, quite assuredly, worked with me throughout the night; that, yes, he did doze off once or twice but only for a moment or so and he always checked the time, I had been patiently looking at the books, reading, writing and occasionally discussing them with him throughout. The work was so absorbing that one hardly was aware of time passing.

"Now who could possibly suspect poor Mrs Cole?

"And the witnesses who had seen Belstrode leave the carousal in the small hours agreed that he was far from incapable when his ordered taxi came for him at 2.30. The pathologist placed Wetton's death at between 2am and 3.30. So Wetton was dead when I crept up the stairs. Because Belstrode was already in the sleep of intoxicated exhaustion.

"Poor Belstrode. Even I could not help but feel sorry for him as he fished for words in the dock. The evidence was so damning. He stoutly denied knowing anything. But when asked if he could be sure he could not have done the murder unawares and his fuddled memory had wiped out all recollection, his strenuous assertions only flew in the face of the medical evidence given. And yet he stubbornly refused to change his plea.

"So followed an adverse summing-up from the judge, a six-hour discussion by the jury and a verdict of guilty. And Belstrode had to look at a judge donning the black cap and pronouncing sentence of death. While his mouth opened and shut and fatuous, useless cries of 'I didn't, I couldn't . . . I wasn't' faintly echoed round the silent court-room.

"I did what I could to lighten his last days in the condemned cell. I lent him *Weir of Hermiston* to read. It was returned to me after the execution. He did not get far with it. Only up to page 54, as it happened.

"There was a great deal of public anger at the verdict. Many people felt there was not a good enough case to take a man's life with. But the jury and the judge thought there was, and the Home Secretary would not reprieve him. So Belstrode died, a few months only after Wetton. A racing man, I suppose, would call it an Autumn Double."

At this point, old Pearson stopped again. He looked at us. As one we stared back. Outside, I remember, light summer rain started to fall.

"That wasn't fair," said Tracey Purvis out loud. "Nobody gave what's-his-name, Belstrode, a chance."

"I do not propose to enter into a discussion, girl," said old Pearson.

That finished that. So for a few moments more he looked at us and we looked at him and nobody said a word. We wondered if he'd finished.

He must have read our thoughts.

"No, I have not yet finished," he said.

He cleared his throat and went on.

"When I started this story I was not sure I could go through with it. I knew in my mind I had to, but not in my heart. Now I know I must finish it, for ever.

"You see, – all those policemen, those lawyers, that judge, that jury; how stupid they all were. So sure they had the truth because it all seemed so obvious. Why did nobody push that senile old clergyman, make him admit that he was an ancient dodderer helplessly asleep in his easy chair all night, who didn't know a thing? Why did they jump to the conclusion that if Belstrode's fingerprints were on the doorhandle attached to Wetton's door then Belstrode must have opened it?"

Pearson's voice had lost some of its calmness. He was beginning to shout. Perhaps in a minute or two he might start stammering again.

Perhaps he thought so too, because now he got a grip on himself again.

"Well," he said. "Let me get it off my chest."

Now we really were staring at him.

"It was very interesting that night in the Vicarage. The old man snored away: I fiddled with his books for a while, then read *Weir of Hermiston* – the first fifty-four pages. Then, at midnight, I turned all the clocks in his room back to five past eleven, did the same to my watch and – very delicately – to his as well. Then I shook him gently and, as he woke, I jumped to the other side of the room and pretended to be at work.

"'Dear me,' he said and looked at his watch. 'I seem to have dozed off for a moment. Did you telephone your landlady?'

"'I have just come back from the phone,' I said.

"'Good,' he replied and went to sleep again.

"I did the same thing to the poor old fool at five-minute intervals four more times. Each time I turned all the clocks on about twenty minutes – so he thought he was waking up of his own accord and so afterwards had no real

91

recollection of sleep. Then I let him sleep for a good long stretch – until two o'clock. Then I put all the clocks and watches forward to 2.45am and woke him up again.

"'It's a quarter to three,' I whispered.

"He looked at his watch. 'Good heavens, so it is,' he said.

"'I must be going,' I said. 'Don't stir. I'll let myself out.'

"'Goodnight, David,' said the old man and drifted back into sleep.

"I put all the clocks back to 2.00am and tiptoed out of the Vicarage. It was a clear night with a nip of approaching winter in the air. The road was quite deserted. There were no street lamps. I moved darkly and quite unobserved.

"At a quarter past two I reached Mrs Cole's house. Here I stopped and waited. I felt inside my overcoat pocket. Besides *Weir of Hermiston*, there was my key, a screwdriver and a pair of gloves. There was something else as well. A white silk scarf which belonged to Belstrode and which I had slipped from off a hook on his door that afternoon.

"Half past two came: a sudden cacophony of bells from all over Abbasridge. It was time. I opened the front door, stood in the dark hallway listening to the ticking of the clock and looking for the line of light under Wetton's door. I took the scarf in both hands, silently opened his door and watched him for a second as he wrote with furious and oblivious concentration.

"My business with him took a very short time. When it was finished I moved silently back on to the landing and listened. There was no sound – except for a just perceptible even breathing coming from Mrs Cole's room.

"So now I produced the screwdriver. It took no more than ten seconds to loosen the grub screws of the identical doorknobs to Wetton's and Belstrode's rooms, exchange them and tighten the screws again. Such a simple thing. And now everyone would think Belstrode had entered Wetton's room. Yet nobody thought to ask why *he* had not worn gloves.

"Then outside again, to wait. It was now 2.45. Belstrode

was a creature of habit to this extent at least. He knew when to finish his drinking and how to return home. No more than two minutes after I had expected, the taxi drew up, Belstrode got out remarkably steadily, paid his fare and fumbled for his key.

"Ten minutes after he entered the house, I finally let myself in, to go to bed. At three o'clock. And nobody ever knew of my lost hour. The rest I have already told you. Poor Belstrode. All the time he waited in the condemned cell, he could not be *quite* sure that he had not done it. After all, if he had not, who had?"

You could *feel* the silence in the room. Nobody could speak; not even Tracey could repeat, "That wasn't fair."

Did we believe him? I don't really know. Did I? I'm not sure. I suppose he must have wondered what effect he'd had on us. When he spoke again, his stammer had come back.

"Y-you see, I c-couldn't stand Wetton, and I really h-hated Belstrode."

Still he faced our blank faces.

"And I g-got what I wanted. My d-degree. My lifetime of t-t-teaching."

Now one of us did speak. It was Shaun Crystal.

"Look where it's got you," he said.

Outside, the rain fell softly on the bike sheds and the drama block, the council houses and the Industrial Estate.

Pearson looked at Shaun levelly.

"It is what I wanted," he said.

The bell rang.

Everyone jumped. Pearson gathered up his books.

"Goodbye," he said. "Thank you for l-listening. We will p-probably never m-meet again."

Nobody answered him.

He left the classroom clumsily and awkwardly. Not one of us moved.

That's not the end. We all of us just sat there, for I don't know how long. Everybody else had gone home. The

93

cleaners were coming round the school. Suddenly, Shaun remembered something.

"Kevin, you great berk. You recorded him."

"So I did," said Kevin. "The tape's ended. I'll rewind it."

As the whirring noise came from the tape-recorder, Tracey thought of something else.

"Hey," she said, "if we took this round to the police, he'd get life."

"Let sleeping dogs lie," said Shaun. "You didn't hate him that much, did you?"

Suddenly we all felt frightened.

The rewinding had finished.

"I'm starting the replay now," said Kevin and pressed the start button. We all listened.

Nothing.

"Perhaps it starts a bit later on the tape," said Kevin.

Still nothing.

"I'll jump a minute or two. Catch him up in the middle," said Kevin.

He did so. Still nothing.

"You stupid article," said Shaun. "I bet you had your finger on the pause button all the time."

"Perhaps it wasn't recording," said Tracey.

"It *was*," said Kevin desperately. "I know it was." His face was red. "I was checking the recording level all the time. And I wasn't touching the pause button, Shaun. You must think I'm thick or something."

"I do," said Shaun.

But the usual fight didn't happen. We were all too puzzled about why not a single word of old Pearson's confession had ended up on the tape. So we shambled off home, bearing a story nobody would believe unless Pearson told someone else and already wondering whether we'd all somehow dreamt it after all.

I was last out. And I saw something on the table. It was a book: Pearson must have left it. I picked it up: it was an oldish, black-bound, dog-eared sort of book and on the spine it said *Weir of Hermiston: R. Louis Stevenson*. Before I went home I took it round to the staff room to give it back. But they'd all gone and the cleaner was picking up a few sherry glasses the other teachers had had to drink Pearson's health in before he left. So I went home and looked at it there.

One leaf was turned down – it was pages 53 and 54. The last line of page 53 read *On the named morning he was at the*. Over the page on 54 it continued with *place of execution*. Five lines on was written *Then followed the brutal instant of extinction and the paltry dangling of the remains like a broken jumping-jack*.

Someone had underlined all those words in ink which had now faded to brown. And in the same ink he had written, "I know you got me here, Pearson. I don't know how you did it, but may you never forget what you have done. I hope it brings you everything you deserve. J.L.B."

So Pearson was wrong. Belstrode did not think for a moment that he had killed Wetton. He knew who to blame. And Pearson must have known it. In spite of what he'd said.

I was never able to give the book back. They fished old Pearson out of the canal next day. Somehow I wasn't surprised. There was an inquest, of course. The verdict was "Misadventure", whatever that means. None of us told our story. Who would have believed us?

So old Pearson passed on. I suppose Belstrode had a strange sort of revenge after all. All Pearson left to show for it was an old book I don't fancy reading, a blank tape (though there was nothing wrong with it; Kevin recorded the Top Forty on it next week), and a memory I can't get rid of which wakes me up in the middle of the night.

You see, there's something else which worries me about it all. Pearson never went to drink his farewell glass of sherry with the rest of the staff. I suppose they hogged the lot waiting for him and then went home. He'd had a free period before his lesson with us, but nobody had seen him in the staff room. And next day he was hauled out of the canal at three in the afternoon. At the inquest they said he'd definitely been dead in the water for at least twenty-four hours. But at three the day before he'd been starting his lesson with us.

Or had he?

That tape stayed blank.

And I wake up in the night.

Hear My Voice

"Oh, go on, sir. Let's not have the summer concert in the boring old school hall. Let's take it outside."

Mr Wycherley sighed. He was Head of Music and his senior choir was being very stroppy.

"Yeah. Let's get out of this rotten old dump."

"Outside in the sunshine. That's where we ought to be. Like the Kings' Singers in punts floating down the river."

Mr Wycherley had a good-natured revolt on his hands. Privately, he agreed with it. Like most secondary school halls, theirs was hardly the Barbican Centre. Perhaps, while he played for time, sarcasm might be his best weapon.

"Where do you suggest?" he enquired. "Shall we turn the tennis courts into the Hollywood Bowl? String quartets in the long jump pit? I'm always open to sensible suggestions." He ignored the ripple of derisive laughter which greeted the last remark.

"Leo's Tump," said a quiet voice beside him.

"I beg your pardon," said Mr Wycherley.

He looked down to his right, where Colin Chiltern sat at the piano.

"Leo's Tump, sir," said Colin. "It's on Wilcox's farm."

"What on earth is Leo's Tump?" said Mr Wycherley.

There was an immediate buzz of approval from the choir.

"Great idea, Colin."

"That would be *really* good."

"Let's get out there now."

Mr Wycherley tapped with his baton on his music stand for quiet.

"Now," he said, "before we have a mass exodus, will somebody please tell me what Leo's Tump is? Or who Leo Stump is, for that matter."

"It's a little hill, sir," said Colin.

"It's not even that," said a girl in the choir. "It's just a tiny bump. Like a little cape at a bend in the river."

"It's not even a river," said a boy in the basses. "It's only a brook."

"Leo's Tump seems to be getting progressively smaller," said Mr Wycherley. "What is this mysterious quality which makes it so suitable for musical performance?"

Colin spoke.

"It's on this bend in the river," he said. "It's like a grassy bank shaded by willow trees. It's not that small. You could have the whole choir sitting on the grass at the top and the orchestra on the flat bit at the bottom easily. And the audience could sit in the meadow on the other side of the river."

"Marvellous," said Mr Wycherley. "And how are we to get a piano out there? They are quite heavy, you know."

"Actually," said Colin, "we could borrow an electronic piano. The fifth-year rock group have got one. It wouldn't be nearly as heavy. Anyway, they'll be playing too. They wouldn't mind lending it."

Now Mr Wycherley was really sarcastic.

"I see," he said. "I didn't realize Leo's Tump was so eminently suitable. How thoughtful of Nature to provide the willow trees with a 240 volt electricity supply and a sufficiency of 13 amp sockets."

There was more laughter – dutiful this time. "Sir's made a funny," an unidentifiable voice said.

Colin continued patiently and quite seriously. "No trouble. The electricity's dead easy."

Blast Chiltern. Why did he have to be so practical as well as so incredibly talented?

"Go on," said Mr Wycherley. "Amaze me yet again."

"Leo's Tump is on Mr Wilcox's land. It's only a

hundred yards away from his cowsheds and milking stalls. We could easily get some heavy duty extension leads."

"Oh, yes? And what about Mr Wilcox? Does he have a say in all this?"

"He's Karen Wilcox's father," said Colin. "She's in the third year. He's Chairman of the PTA. And he's putting up for the District Council next elections. He'd be dead chuffed about it. It'd get his name known among the voters."

"Ah, well," said Mr Wycherley. "'There is a tide in the affairs of men' as the English Department would say. I'll think about it. And I'll have a word with the Head."

The choir cheered.

"You won't regret it, sir," said Colin.

"All right, then. Settle down." Mr Wycherley was the efficient conductor once again. "From the start. *Non Nobis Domine*."

The choir groaned.

"I'll write something specially for the concert," said Colin. "World première at Leo's Tump."

Yes, thought Mr Wycherley. Colin Chiltern will write something for the concert. And it will be superb. Mr Wycherley felt the pride of the good teacher in a brilliant pupil. And Colin Chiltern was a prodigy. A brilliant pianist, violinist, flautist – and a composer whose mastery of form, harmony, melody, were way beyond his years. Could Mozart have been any more competent at the same age? Mr Wycherley could not see how. Colin Chiltern ought (or so some thought) to be at a specialist music school or the Royal College. But his parents would have none of it. They kept him on at the local comprehensive where he remained happy and well liked in spite of – or perhaps because of – his huge and extraordinary talent.

Brother Leofric's stone cell was cold at the best of times; the quiet morning hours after matins on a snowy, lowering January day meant a particular bone-rotting bitterness for

99

the old monk. Arthritis over the years had crippled his fingers so that it was a wonder he could still hold his brush as he worked painstakingly at the illuminations on the parchment. But what he had lost in dexterity he had kept in cunning and the blinding ropes of colour crept surely across the page as they had always done.

De Profundis. The one hundred and thirtieth psalm. *Out of the deep have I called unto you, O Lord. Lord hear my voice.*

His cracked old voice chanted the words in his beloved Latin. *Lord, hear my voice.*

Brother Leofric was scribe for the monastery. *De Profundis* he was copying: a copy to be the King of all copies and to be presented to the Archbishop himself one day. So the script was the most painstaking and the illuminations were the most intricate, the most colourful, the most beautiful that even he, Brother Leofric of the sure though shaking hand, had ever been responsible for. Which meant it would be unmatched anywhere.

Out of the deep. The words sounded in the cell. *Lord, hear my voice.* The old man in the coarse brown habit sang softly to himself.

De profundis. The reds and greens and golds and purples twined snake-like over the page. The great letter D and the lesser E to start the page took shape. In the middle of the greater letter D under Brother Leofric's cunning hand there began to form a mouth: between its lips, a tongue. *Hear my voice.* Brother Leofric sang again, repetitively. The mouth grew on the parchment.

Colin Chiltern sat at the piano in the living room of his home. A neat pile of manuscript paper rested on top of the piano: loose sheets covered with music were placed carefully on the floor by the stool. He wrote on the sheet before him as he tried melodies, phrases and harmonies. He was very happy.

He had decided what he would write. A four-part unaccompanied anthem for the school choir. In whose style should it be? He surveyed the list of English composers he most admired: Gibbons, Tallis, Byrd, Purcell, Elgar, Britten. All of them and none. Their harmonies filled his mind. But as soon as he put pen to paper he was his own man. The style was of them all, yet it was his own. He had soon decided what words he would use. They were words which – from his earliest years singing in the church choir – had fascinated him. Psalm 130. The first verse and a half only.

> *Out of the deep have I called unto thee, O Lord.*
> *Lord, hear my voice.*
> *Out of the deep:*

What marvellous rising, straining, urgent musical phrases those words conjured up. The deep of what? The deep, dark silent places of the sea? The hidden deeps of the mind? Yes. A rising, repeated figure starting quiet and deep with the basses as if from a formless void: taken up by the tenors and getting louder, faster and clearer but with the basses forming an underlying, satisfying harmony: then on to the altos, faster still and more ornate, with the underlying harmonies now thicker, fuller: finally a climax with the sopranos, spreading over four octaves and culminating in a rich, full statement. His fingers trembled with joy as the notes spread across the manuscript paper; his mind exulted as he reproduced an interior performance which could fill the Albert Hall or make the echoes ring for miles and miles around Leo's Tump. And that other phrase. *Hear my voice.* What a superb three words they were. He turned them in his mind into a multitude of quick three-note phrases, tossed from bass to tenor, tenor to soprano, soprano back down to alto like a flowing passing movement in a football match.

Yes, his anthem would be wonderful. A beautiful object made from nothing. No one else could do it.

It's quite extraordinary, thought Mr Wycherley. Those kids couldn't be more right. Leo's Tump was even better than they had described. The sweep of the little river, the promontory which was the Tump itself, the sloping, concave lie of the meadow opposite, all combined to turn the place into a natural amphitheatre. Now he had seen it, he was full of the idea.

Mr Wilcox had been very co-operative. He had offered car-parking in the next field, full use of the electricity supply in his cowsheds as well as his own heavy-duty extension leads and all the rehearsal time on the Tump the school needed.

"All you want now is the weather," he said.

"The place is so perfect that if we don't get the right weather on the night, we'll wait till we do," said Mr Wycherley.

The two men stood on the top of the Tump looking down the river.

"Why is it called Leo's Tump?" asked Mr Wycherley.

"No one rightly knows," said Mr Wilcox. "I think it's something to do with the old monastery."

"I didn't know there was one," said Mr Wycherley.

"It's gone, years ago. You can still see the earthworks and a few old stones two miles down-stream."

"But why Leo?"

"I did hear once an old story about some monk called Leo who managed to raise the devil."

"So?"

"They're both under the Tump."

"I hope they never get out," said Mr Wycherley.

The two men walked together away from the Tump and down to the pub.

Leofric's cell was very small: the stone walls were feet thick. The grey misty light which filtered in through the high glassless window gave little light: sometimes being in the cell was like sitting in a tiny box at the centre of the earth.

So when Leofric heard an echo to his cracked old voice as it sang its little plainsong refrain over and over again

102

while his hands worked busily he said to himself, "Strange. I have heard echoes in the chapel and the refectory and even outside among the hills. But never in my cell."

And all the while, the mouth with its lips and its tongue took shape. And the echo grew most distinct. *Hear my voice.*

It was not an echo. It was a separate voice.

The mouth was complete. Its lips were curved, hooked, cruel. Its tongue was barbed, like a serpent told of in some traveller's tale.

Hear my voice. Hear my voice. The voice was shrill, demented, biting deep into Brother Leofric's mind. He dropped his brush, placed his hands over his ears and stared at the complete mouth that had appeared on the page through his cunning hand but which he had never, never intended.

Hear my voice.

The little cell was full of deafening sound. He clapped his hands even tighter to his ears. To no avail.

He screamed to drown the noise but could not even hear himself. He bent downward to pick the parchment up. It seemed to crackle back at him with a force of its own. Shooting pains entered his fingers and ran along his arms. He staggered out of his cell holding the parchment in front of him like a shield. His sandals flapped over the stones and his fellow monks emerged from their cells or stopped their work outside to stare strangely at him.

"What have I done?" he cried. "Have I been too proud?"

The voice beat on in his hears. *Hear my voice. Hear my voice.* But no other monk came over to Leofric: no other monk gave any sign of having heard it. Brother Leofric stumbled on, out of the monastery, over the snow-covered land to the dark river and then along its bank towards the hills far away.

I will lift up my eyes to the hills. His mind wanted him to chant the words to combat the hideous, hideous *hear my*

103

voice. But his vocal cords could not move: he made no sounds beyond retching gasps for breath.

The weather at the end of June looked as though it was set fair for weeks. The first rehearsals at Leo's Tump showed even more clearly how good it was as an open-air theatre. Already there was talk of *A Midsummer Night's Dream* being put on there next year. Everything was rehearsed to perfection at the Tump – except *Out of the Deep* by Colin Chiltern. The choir had practised it until they could sing it in their sleep. But Colin was adamant. The first performance was to be at Leo's Tump and it was to be the only one. His purist ear wanted to savour the particular sound of *Out of the Deep* in the open air to the accompaniment of the murmuring river just once and never again.

Back at school, though, the anthem had shaped well. The choir loved it and sang it with special affection because they knew it was written entirely for them and that it was music quite out of the ordinary.

The day approached. The weather stayed clear and hot. Chairs were brought up from the school and put in rows in the meadow. Music stands for the orchestra were set up on the little beach at the foot of the Tump. The extension leads were laid for the rock group (who weren't quite happy about the arrangement) and for the electronic piano.

Mr Wycherley watched it all happen under his direction and crossed his fingers. The logistics of setting up the concert each year were bad enough normally: he must have needed his head examined to make it all ten times worse. But if it went off well, wouldn't it be something to remember?

Well, he hoped so. But it would be Colin's night really. It was Colin's idea, and the centrepiece of the whole evening would be Colin's anthem. Mr Wycherley, in spite of himself, could not repress a pang of envy. By heck, that Colin Chiltern was a lucky one.

* * *

Hear my voice. The screaming, demented voice was changing. It grew quieter.

"Thank God," breathed Brother Leofric.

It settled down to a whisper. But what a whisper. A whisper deep in the inner ear, so raw and rasping that it seemed to gouge out the eardrum. And what a feeling accompanied it. For the words that were whispered in his ear and the mouth that whispered them seemed to belong to something that sat on the back of his neck, that squatted on his shoulders. Nothing was there: he *knew* nothing could be there. But this nothing was heavy; it weighed him down, it made him stop, stumble, lose his footing in the snow.

What had happened? Part of Brother Leofric's mind could still work clearly: it reasoned well and came up with the only answer. He had to tell everyone.

He turned.

Before him, watching him wonderingly but not leaving the precincts of the monastery, stood the monks. Leofric made a superhuman effort and his voice carried with desperate strength across the grey snow, almost as if the words he spoke were illumined on the parchment-grey breath which came from his mouth.

"Listen. Listen, my brothers. With my own art I have raised the fiend. Rather your hands should lose their cunning than you should raise him too."

Leofric turned again and moved, now with awful slowness, through the snow towards the far hills.

The evening of the concert was here. The weather stayed perfect. Lines of cars drew up in the field Mr Wilcox had given for parking; the rows of seats in the meadow filled up with shirt-sleeved and summer-dressed parents and friends. The girls of the choir and orchestra arrived in their long dresses; the boys filed to their places in their dark grey trousers and white shirts. To Mr Wycherley, moving to the conductor's stand for Schubert's *Marche Militaire*, the whole scene looked comfortingly familiar yet – framed by the willow trees, the far hills and the blue sky, the audience separated from the performers by a running river – uneasily different.

Leofric could go no further. The weight of whatever thing it was gripping the back of his neck and whispering in his ear was too much to bear. He sank to his knees and wept.

Then, above the whispering, he heard a voice shouting from far off.

"Leofric. Leofric."

With his last strength, he turned. A burly figure, also in a brown habit, was running towards him, leaving untidy footprints in the wet snow. With a leap of the heart, Leofric recognized him. It was his Abbot. In him, thought Leofric, I put my trust.

"What is happening, old friend?"

Leofric looked up at the Abbot with piteous eyes.

"The fiend," he whispered.

Could the Abbot see what Leofric felt on the back of his neck? Leofric did not know. But the Abbot's eyes showed understanding.

"Come on, old friend. Back to the monastery."

"No," gasped Leofric. "I must carry this scourge far away."

"Then I will come with you."

The Abbot looped his huge arm round Leofric's thin shoulders and pulled him on his way. He saw the parchment manuscript with the mouth on it but said nothing. They trudged on.

He stopped suddenly, and Leofric stopped with him. They stood on a little hill which overlooked a bend in the river. All around them was deserted whiteness.

"Stop here, Leofric," said the Abbot. "Lay down your burden."

Out of the deep was the last item of the concert. When he had come to arrange the programme, Mr Wycherley could think of no more fitting finale. Colin stood alone at the conductor's stand, facing his singers. He played the commencing note; then raised his arms to bring the basses in and start the deep rhythmic murmur which set the anthem in motion.

"I cannot," said Leofric. "I cannot lay it down. The burden is with me for ever."

He felt the grip of the thing on the back of his neck tighten even further: the whispering kept on and on.

"Then I will help you, Leofric," said the Abbot.

He faced Leofric, looking him square in the eyes. He made the sign of the cross and then cried out in Latin the great prayer of exorcism.

The whispering in Leo's ear stopped. It changed again – to a scream, without words, which rose shrilly. The grip tightened – but its feel was changed, as if now the thing was clinging on desperately.

The anthem reached its halfway point. The opening words – *Out of the deep have I called unto thee, Oh Lord* – had ended in that full, rich affirmative chord Colin's fingers had trembled to write. The sound of his own music was such that the back hairs on his scalp rose and tears of joy welled at the back of his eyes.

Now the chasing three-note figure of the words *Hear my voice* were to start the final part. His ears almost ached with the anticipation of hearing his work again.

Leofric listened. Quiet at first but growing louder came a strange, full, unearthly music such as he had never heard. In the background he could hear the Abbot still chanting the prayer of exorcism, casting out the unclean spirit. But the new music soon flooded his being and he stared down in wonder to the river from where it seemed to come. There a figure mistily stood: a figure in black and white, around whom the music seemed to radiate.

The intricate, extraordinary sounds floated round Brother Leofric's mind like a patterned design. The different melodies took on colours to him. The girls' high voices were a bright gold: the girls' lower notes were a warm red. The high men's notes were a fierce sky blue: the bass voices a rich purple. The coloured ropes of sound twined round his brain until Colin Chiltern's anthem heard from over the centuries turned into one of his own illuminations.

The thing on the back of his neck loosened its grip. And now Leofric heard words in the music – *Hear my voice* – and he knew what would happen. The thing detached itself from his neck. For the first time he saw it, squat, slime-green, foul. And it hopped obscenely towards its new prize, the misty figure in black and white, while its renewed whispers of *Hear my voice* seemed to merge with that sweet music.

They had reached the final cadences. As the music swept all round him, Colin closed his eyes, making the notes a disembodied, pure sound. But with his eyes closed he saw a different sight in front of him. The Tump was still there – but on it were two brown-habited men. One clasped his hands together and seemed to be shouting at the sky. The other, nearer, was old. He stared straight at Colin, a beseeching fear in his eyes. And on the back of his neck sat a loathsome creature, slime-green and scaly, with black, dead eyes and a mouth with hooked and cruel lips and a barbed tongue.

Time seemed to stop. The anthem froze in his mind. No longer was it something which moved from beginning to end in the space of four minutes. He saw it all at once, like an intricate design, the melodies like twining, coloured lines, making a delicately shaped framework with a space in the middle.

Through the space he could see the old man with the creature on his back. And when the framework was complete, the creature left the old man and hopped towards him. The dead eyes looked at him, the barbed tongue flicked, the mouth whispered, *Hear my voice*.

The sound bit into Colin's ears. He felt claws dig hard into his shoulders and neck as the creature took up its place. Colin staggered under the weight: he seemed to lose balance. It was as if a sudden roaring sheet of flame engulfed him and he was hurled into a deep abyss.

The Abbot thought they had been struck by lightning. He reeled under the simultaneous blinding flash and reverberating clap and then stared incredulously at the great crack in the ground which appeared at his feet. He looked at Leofric, who lay on the ground, a look almost of peace in his eyes.

"It has left me," the old man said.

The parchment he had carried all this time lay beside him. A sudden gust of wind lifted it: down into the fissure it fluttered and lay there, four feet deep with the painted mouth facing upward.

"Where has the fiend gone to?" asked Leofric.

"I do not know," said the Abbot.

"I brought him forth." Leofric tried to rise, then sank back. "I thought my gifts raised me above other men. So he came to me."

He lay still, his eyes open and staring. The Abbot watched for a moment, then bent down and gently closed the lids.

"Now, old friend," he said, "This is your resting place. You must be left with the companion you brought into the world. I cannot take you back with me to our holy ground."

He cradled the old, dead man in his arms and laid him in the crack in the ground.

"Goodbye, Leofric," he said. "We will come back to give you proper burial."

Nobody was ever sure what happened as the anthem reached its end. Some said there must have been a shaft of summer lightning which sprang without warning from the sky and struck Colin down as the last chord of his great anthem sounded through the air. Others said the strain of seeing the concert right through to the end was too much for him and he had a mild stroke. At any rate, without warning, he staggered, fell and lay unconscious while the choir rushed round him and Mr Wilcox ran as hard as he could to the house to ring for an ambulance. In their horror, all the members of the audience forgot the beauty of the anthem, though afterwards they would recall it with burning clarity.

A month passed. Colin had been very ill. Now he was up and about again, but he seemed to have a stoop which indicated that he might indeed have suffered a slight stroke. Today, for the first time since before the concert, he sat at his piano. He placed some manuscript paper on the table by his side. He was going to compose again.

He opened his mind to let the music in and his hands rested on the piano keys. He was aware of a weight on the back of his neck, as of something he could not see but knew always to be there, ready at his ear to whisper.

And slowly the music came. It came in discords and it came in deep gruff snatches which could not be called melodies. It came in howls and shrieks as from some dark and secret place of terror. It came without beauty and without joy, as if telling truths which he could not understand but which he had to express. It filtered its way out of his mind through his fingers on to the keys and then into notes on the manuscript paper so that the truths were frozen for ever. And it came compulsively and with an unreasoning power, to be written down at once, though every note that jerked itself from him was hard and bitter agony.

The weather changed. A windy, cold summer gave way to an early, dark autumn. Mr Wycherley grieved for his pupil.

He missed the joy of seeing the long, clean-nailed fingers scamper across the piano keys; of finding on the neatly scribed manuscript paper marvellous music no one had heard before; of talk with one who knew instinctively what he himself had spent his whole life learning. Surely that superb mind had not been made to stop growing? Now there was just a tall boy with a stoop and dark eyes deep and morose. There was no talking, no laughter.

For month upon month, Mr Wycherley mused. What had struck Colin down? No answer came. Then, one night in February, he remembered. What had Mr Wilcox said that summer day? "They're both under the Tump." Yes, that was it. And one of them had got out. Was that crazy? No crazier than Colin coming to consciousness with all his music gone.

All that week he watched the silent, closed-up Colin Chiltern. He remembered the great ones of the past; Mozart and Schubert, dead in their prime, Beethoven so deaf he never heard his greatest work. And what about John Keats? Mr Wycherley thought of noble poets in their misery dead.

Yes, he knew what had happened to Colin Chiltern. And perhaps it had to.

Mr Wycherley never quite knew what made him, that raw Sunday afternoon in February, put on his walking boots and cagoule and set out across the fields to Leo's Tump.

It was different now. The fields were muddy and squelched underfoot where melted snow and heavy rain had not drained away. The river itself flowed high and brown. The cows huddled together for warmth and the willow trees no longer bent over protectively but gestured in the stiff wind as if warning him off.

He stood below the Tump, on what was left above water of the little beach where he had conducted only last summer. He tried to see in his mind's eye the orchestra and choir and lifted his hands as if to set them off. But it was difficult to imagine music in this desolate place and all at once he felt foolish.

He was being watched. A dark figure in jeans, roll-neck

111

jersey and donkey jacket was sitting under a willow tree, its back against the trunk, hands clasped round knees. It spoke.

"You won't hear the music and neither will I."

Whatever is Colin doing at the Tump? thought Mr Wycherley. Does he come here regularly? Why?

"You will hear it, Colin," he said. "You will hear it again."

Colin looked down on his teacher. You know nothing, he thought. You can't help me. No one can. Week after week I come here, to see if this thing will get off my back and go where it came from. If it doesn't go of its own accord I am past helping.

Mr Wycherley scrambled up the slope. Colin answered him without moving.

"I will never hear the music again," he said.

Mr Wycherley squatted down beside him.

"You will, Colin, you will," he said.

Colin turned dark eyes towards him but said nothing.

"Colin. I *know* what got out of the ground and entered your soul."

No answer.

"Colin, tell me. Is the music just a noise? Just a rackety row?"

No answer again. But Colin's hands round his knees showed white as they gripped each other harder.

"And more than that. Do people you liked seem hateful? Is the world suddenly ugly? Cruel? Hopeless?

No answer again. But the eyes widened.

"I'm right, aren't I, Colin? You don't need to say a word; I know I am. But this comes to everybody in the end, Colin. We all know sooner or later what the world is like. But it's come early to you. It's come before your time and without warning. It's hit you deep down inside and you can't sort it out."

Colin spoke at last. His voice was thick and weary.

"Why me?"

Mr Wycherley's voice was urgent. Now he knew what to say.

"Colin, you're different from the rest of us. You can see further and deeper than other people. One day your music will speak for them. You had harmony; now you've got noise. But the music can't die. The world has sorrow, yes, but the joy's still there. Keep listening to the noise, Colin. You'll make your art from the world as it is, not how you'd like it to be."

Colin listened – both to Mr Wycherley and to his own mind. No, it was still noise. He closed his eyes.

He still seemed to see the Tump and the river below it. Two figures stood there. One was very tall and strongly built. The other stooped and was old. Both wore brown habits. They turned and looked at him.

Mr Wycherley still spoke and Colin still heard him.

"Keep listening to the noise. It will turn into music."

The old man spoke as well.

"We have come back, Colin. That other time was not the end. I did not want to pass the fiend on to you. Better that he should have stayed with me. Forgive me, Colin."

Then the Abbot spoke.

"A good man lies here," he said. "We gave him proper burial. So where you sit is holy ground. The fiend will hurt you sorely. But he cannot conquer you. Hear *my* voice, Colin."

Colin opened his eyes.

"Yes," he said. "I shall listen."

He rose and walked away, without looking back. As he walked, he listened. Inside his mind the noise changed. The old harmonies did not return. But out of the cacophony there came, dimly at first but steadily stronger, a deeper, stranger music than he had ever heard before. He did not understand it; was not sure if he could handle it. But his pace quickened and soon he broke into a run, to lose no time in trying to capture it for ever.

Fraternal Greetings

Silent in the dark night the tall ship stood at anchor, lifting and settling gently in the slight swell. No riding lights were lit, not a match or a lamp flickered on board. Had it been day, the sails could not have been seen black as ink, matching the tarry blackness of the hull. But now, in the dead of night, the ship merged into the shades, swaying gently, expectantly.

Crouched under the tarpaulin of a lifeboat was a man. His long discomfort was about to end. In a few minutes he would commit a murder. He waited for the sound of footsteps on the deck.

Sir James Blackhull had built up the famous Blackhull shipping line from nothing. Once his earliest struggles were over, he never went to sea himself. Sailors in their hundreds toiled all over the oceans, lived out their hard and frugal lives and often drowned for him. He sat behind his desk in his panelled boardroom and grew richer and richer.

A Blackhull Line ship, with its great press of ink-black sails, was a disturbing sight. Distinctive by day like a mark of Cain on the high seas, at night it could fade away and go where perhaps it should not. For Sir James Blackhull was not particular how his fortune was built up. If a rival ship-owner went bankrupt, Sir James would be there to take over his business – almost as if he knew it would happen. If a coffin-ship sank with all hands, perhaps Sir James would happen to grow a little richer. If in some faraway country rebels cried out for arms, a black-sailed ship might silently arrive in a deserted creek. Its cargo of rifles, carbines and ammunition would be unloaded at the very same time a sister ship would disgorge an identical cargo in the main port for the government forces. Whoever won, Sir James kept his friends, knowing his enemies would be shot by guns he had supplied himself.

Sir James had two sons, Jasper and Roderick. His wife died bearing their still-born third child. So only his sons and the Line were left to live for. James schooled Jasper and Roderick well. The same ruthlessness, the same wish to cut out everybody who got in the way – these he passed on to Jasper, so when he died the Blackhull Line was left to the elder son intact and assured of no change in direction.

But Sir James had passed the same qualities on to Roderick – and he was the younger son who had to play second fiddle. This was something Roderick did not like.

For three years the brothers worked outwardly peaceably. Indeed, for Jasper, the peace was complete. He wheeled and dealed, cheated and prospered just as his father had done. The business grew, and the villainy with it. Roderick did his part: Jasper daily renewed his approval of as great a blackguard, so he thought, as himself. Never did he think his younger brother a greater blackguard.

But all this time, what was Roderick thinking of? In his mind was a consuming jealousy. Whose was the final decision in everything? Jasper's. Who took the credit for each coup, each mean triumph? Jasper. Not Roderick, though he had schemed as much, been as cunning, been as ruthless. Jasper's was the credit because Jasper's was the power and Jasper's the responsibility.

And on a bright June morning in 1874 Roderick suddenly knew what to do.

Roderick was sitting in his father's old leather-upholstered chair behind his father's huge oak desk. Jasper stood at the great round window which overlooked the quayside where the barquentine *Boreas* was tied up, black sails furled, as the cargo of coffee-beans was

115

unloaded. Roderick watched the sunlight stream in, making his brother's fair hair seem almost to catch fire.

Jasper spoke.

"Coffee-beans." he said, "Coffee-beans. A difference from the cargo she will take out, Roderick. Yes?"

The bottom of the circular window was actually at floor level. Where Jasper stood, the whole of him was visible to anyone on the quay who cared to look up. Suddenly, with a flash of mental light as bright as that which reflected off Jasper's hair, Roderick realized that merely by rising to his feet, taking four steps and charging with his square, stocky shoulders, he would become sole master of the Blackhull Line. For Jasper would be sprawled, broken, on the pavement underneath, surrounded by shattered glass and jagged window-frame.

That, though, would be crude and dangerous. Perhaps even he could not buy off the law.

Jasper spoke again.

"In four days' time at high tide the *Boreas* sails. Cast-iron lampposts for the streets of Mexico City, the Bill of Lading says. But we know what the cargo really is, do we not, brother?"

"Maxim guns to mow down the Emperor," murmured Roderick, almost bored. Villainy soon became routine.

"I shall sail with her," said Jasper. "I must see there is no mistake."

Then there was the second flash of light in Roderick's mind. With no conscious premeditation, he said, "I shall sail for New York tomorrow."

"Why?" said Jasper.

"To see MacCluskey. To get his business. If I go unknown, unannounced, I can secure the contract. Our rivals will not know." His voice was very quiet and matter-of-fact. "Not even you shall know which ship I sail on. MacCluskey will give in. We will win as always."

"Good," said Jasper and, thinking no more of it, watched the stevedores swarm in and out of the *Boreas*. Roderick looked at his brother with pitying contempt.

116

Next day he left the house as if for a journey. But he never travelled a mile. When the *Boreas* sailed on Thursday, both brothers were on board. One was in the stateroom in comfort. The other crouched for days on end having stowed away in a lifeboat, feeling that the danger and the hideous discomfort were worth all that he had decided to do.

Two miles out from the Central American coast, waiting for rebels to fetch their illicit cargo, the *Boreas* rose and fell in the warm breeze off the land. Under the tarpaulin beside Roderick were the last of his provisions, which he had just eked out over the Atlantic, a bag containing clothes for a more respectable life and – next to his compulsively opening and shutting hand – a corked bottle and rag. And seven leaden weights.

All lights were dowsed. All hands were below, waiting. Roderick strained his ears for the steps he knew so well. Jasper would take his last walk round the deck, as every night. The last of the night: now, the last of his life.

Tlip, tlip, tlip. Leather soles on the shiny, smooth wooden deck. Tlip, tlip, nearer, nearer. Roderick uncorked his bottle; soaked the rag in it. Tlip, tlip – now by the boat. And silently Roderick rose, a wraith, black upon black, behind his brother. The chloroform-soaked rag over Jasper's mouth and nose; the weights deep down in his pockets; the limp body heaved over the side; Roderick, carrying bag and leaving no trace behind, diving in after it and swimming with strong, smooth strokes without a splash for the shore, out of sight and hearing before the first wondering sailor ran to the rail in mystification.

A fortnight later, a dark-haired, dapper-suited man reached New York, did hard business with MacCluskey and set sail homeward for England, there to be desolated by news of his elder brother's disappearance and presumed drowning.

Now everything was Roderick's.

* * *

117

Jasper's body was never found. But the evidence given by crew members seemed conclusive enough: death by drowning was presumed. And three months later Roderick stood, dark and inscrutable, at a memorial service to his brother in the half-empty cathedral, listening to a droning encomium from the Dean.

"'They that go down to the sea in ships' is indeed a convenient text," came the insistent clerical voice.

Old fool, thought Roderick, not a muscle or eyelid moving in his face.

"For though our dearly beloved brother here departed seldom went down to the sea in ships himself yet if others had not done so for him we would not have gathered here to honour his memory. For his substance, his probity, his worth to our community was gained by those who toiled over the oceans on his behalf."

Roderick's eyes narrowed. Was this priest uttering veiled digs at the Blackhull Line? But there seemed no change in the Dean's voice and the rest of the congregation was nodding in wise agreement. For what the sermon was saying was after all how the world was run and always would be.

"And perhaps we can see the hand of our Lord in our dear brother's death."

Roderick stiffened. What was this man going to say?

"For he lived by the sea: one might even say he lived off the sea. Seldom, because of the great weight of responsibilities that he bore, did he go *on* the sea. It is perhaps oddly fitting that, having just this once done so, he should be now lying *in* the sea."

A sudden almost superstitious fear ran through Roderick's body. This stupid clergyman in his fatuous sermon seemed to be trying to ferret something out: as if he knew there was a truth to be goaded from him. Roderick turned and looked at the rest of the congregation: sober, grave, dark-suited, well-fed – lawyers, bankers, factory-owners, other shipowners; associates, rivals, enemies; all looking back at the Dean's opening and shutting mouth with glazed indifference.

118

Yes, if the Dean was trying out some strange humour of his own, it was lost on these gathered worthies. Roderick fell to musing again, working out in his mind a new plan to gain business and do down rivals.

"Death by water is a cleansing death".

The Dean's words captured Roderick's attention again. The sermon was finishing. Soon the congregation would rise, the organist would crash out the introductory chords and the choir would lead the congregation in "Eternal Father, strong to save". But those words stuck in Roderick's mind.

"Death by water is a cleansing death."

And as he thought about and heard in his mind the Dean saying it, the voice seemed changed. It was not the Dean's voice any more. It was another voice. One he knew.

Throughout the hymn he stood silent. At the end he strode out of the cathedral, speaking to no one.

That night he slept badly.

Next day was fine. Roderick's high spirits returned. He strode along the quay watching with the pride of complete possession the loading and unloading of the *Boreas*, the *Orphion* and the *Eurynome*. He nodded patronisingly to those who called greetings to him. Now he was truly the Blackhull Line.

After an hour or so he went up to the great office, passing lines of clerks busy with the administration of so vast an enterprise. He sat behind his father's oaken desk, knowing that now he was there by right. Before him was the huge circular window before which Jasper had once stood when the deadly plan had flashed into his mind.

Yes, Jasper had stood there and the sun, pouring in, had reflected in golden light off his straw-coloured hair – just as it was doing now.

Roderick jerked himself out of his reverie. That was ridiculous. The sun could not reflect off nothing. Yet at head height was a golden luminosity, as if something was

119

sending the sun's rays back. Despite himself, Roderick thought of fair, washed hair and the words of yesterday came into his mind: "Death by water is a cleansing death."

With an effort he put the sight and the voice out of his mind. There was work to be done and Roderick Blackhull would do it.

An hour later he gave up. Concentration was impossible. He stalked out of the office and, ordering the clerks to tell callers he had left town, he wandered the streets till nightfall.

That night he dreamed. He heard the sermon in the cathedral again – or something like it, for it sounded in his ears like droning gibberish. But the Dean's face he could not distinguish – except that strangely it seemed surrounded by fair hair which shone in the sunlight. The last words, though, he heard without difficulty.

"Death by water is a cleansing death."

The voice was not the Dean's. It was, piercingly clearly, Jasper's.

In the morning, the manservant knocked discreetly on the bedroom door. He entered at Roderick's command, bearing towels and a large jug of hot water which he poured into the washbasin.

When the servant had left Roderick stood in his night-shirt in front of the basin, about to plunge his hands into the steaming liquid. "Water is cleansing," said a voice deep inside his mind.

He withdrew his hands and backed away from the basin, staring at it.

Walking along the quayside, he could see, beyond the twin breakwaters of the harbour, the hard grey line of the horizon. It seemed to press in on him, as if he could stretch out his hand, past toy sailing ships and a lighthouse looking in the daylight like a dead match, to touch its oppressive definiteness. Sea met sky not three feet away from his eyes, so it seemed – yet for the first time in his life its suffocating vastness chilled his heart and made his head swim.

He fled into the office and sat breathlessly behind the great desk.

There was no sun that day, so even if Jasper had been there to stand in front of the window, light would not have reflected off his yellow hair. So what was the shining shape Roderick made out just where Jasper had stood when his death was resolved upon?

Something three-dimensional hung there at head height and shone of its own accord. Roderick blinked. He willed it to disappear. It disappeared. With a mirthless laugh, in bitter experimentation, he willed it back again. It reappeared. With a grunt of triumph he willed it to disapear.

It stayed where it was.

Roderick sat bowed forward with his head in his hands and did no work that day.

That night, Roderick lay sleepless for hours, staring at the ceiling. Could it possibly be that something had returned to haunt him? Or was there some silly quirk inside his own brain which was making him think in ways he would prefer no to? He certainly could not be having guilt feelings. He had never felt guilty about anything in the whole of his life.

It was four in the morning before he slept. And when he slept, he dreamt. He dreamt he saw his brother's face, rippling as though clear running water flowed over it, with light fair hair lifting and falling gently.

His brother smiled and his lips moved. Though coming from under water the words he spoke sounded quite clear.

"I died by water. So will you."

In his dream, Roderick found himself able to speak.

"Where have you come from?"

The watery smiling face answered.

"You brought me back. You sent me away and you brought me back. You laid in wait for me and now you have brought me back to lie in wait for you."

There was silence. Then the mouth moved again.

"I died by water. So will you."

And faded away.

Roderick's sleep became dreamless and deep. When he woke, the dream was just a nagging discomfort at the back of his mind. Later, once again behind the desk, he daringly willed the formless, glistening shape that had yesterday been in front of the window to return. Dutifully it came back, but when Roderick willed it away again, it stayed stubbornly where it was. And then Roderick remembered his dream in every little detail.

Roderick never felt lonely now he lived on his own in the house left by his father. This was not surprising: he had not felt any companionship when his father and brother were alive. Roderick prided himself on being quite self-contained. His domestic staff existed only to look after him; he did not recognize them as people.

When he pondered, therefore, on what was happening to him, he pondered alone. When a thought came into his mind there was no one to criticize it, to counter it, to place another idea beside it. The thought was free to grow, to swell unchecked, to obliterate everything round it, like a cancer.

The thought that now filled his mind was that somehow his dead brother had come back to trouble him. What alternative was there? Could Jasper perhaps not have drowned and was here in the flesh? Impossible. Roderick *knew* he had killed him. Besides, if Jasper were really alive, he would appear in the office in front of the desk, not in a dream under clear water. And in the dream, Jasper had said, "You brought me back". What could that mean? Surely dreams came from within the mind, not from outside. Who, then, was speaking? Jasper? Or Roderick himself?

"You brought me back." Yes – and if that were true he could send his brother away again. Of course – the shining shape in the office. He could will it to come and go away again. But not always. This morning it had stayed.

That did not count. He was only experimenting. A real mental effort would send his hauntings away for ever.

There was a knock at the door.

"What is it?" called Roderick.

An obsequious voice answered.

"Your bath is ready, sir."

The manservant opened the door and Roderick strode through, to where the bathtub stood, filled to the top with steaming water.

What bliss, to relax in it, to lie back and close one's eyes, forgetting all the day's worries, to doze, to slip under . . . to drown. Roderick recalled what else his dream-brother had said. "I died by water. So will you."

He spoke aloud to the empty room.

"No. I will not be trapped by you. You cannot lie in wait for me: I will see you wherever you care to hide."

He ran back to his room and locked the door.

Now, he could take careful and rational stock of his situation. Jasper plainly meant what he had said. The dead brother was determined to take revenge by ensuring he died by water. There were therefore two possible courses of action. First, he must rid himself of his dead brother. Second, he must keep himself away at all costs from water. He weighed both ideas and found them sensible and intelligent. Greatly cheered, he went to bed and slept soundly until morning.

When he rose, it occurred to him for the first time what keeping away from water would mean. The manservant was dismissed with orders to take the washbasin and jug away and destroy them. Later, sweaty and unshaven, Roderick entered the office, having crept along the walls of the buildings lining the quayside to keep as great a distance as possible between

123

himself and the sea. The clerks in the outer office looked at him strangely as he entered: as always, he was not aware of them.

Behind the desk he sat, stretching out his arms and laying them on the smooth and shiny oak top. There was so much work to be done – work that had been forgotten during these last fearful days. But now he knew what to do, all his energies would soon be devoted to the greater glory of the Blackhull Line.

He looked towards the circular window. Yes, the shining reflection was there again. Once again, he experimented.

"Go away," he said.

It disappeared.

"Come back."

It was there again.

"What are you?" said Roderick.

Somehow he was not surprised when the shape expanded, downwards, into misty human form and stood there as Jasper, rippling as if under water.

"So you are really here," said Roderick. "Well, I know how to deal with you. I shall not die by water because I shall never touch water, I shall never see water, I will never go near water. Water will no longer be a part of my life. So it cannot possibly be part of my death."

Jasper stood and smiled as he had in the dream.

"And as for you," continued Roderick, "I can be rid of you at any time. I called you up: I willed you here. Now I will you to go away again."

Jasper still stood there, in front of the great round window.

Nonplussed, Roderick thought furiously. Then he remembered his immediate thought the first time he had resolved to rid himself of Jasper. Then he had thought of charging at him and knocking him through the window to the pavement beneath. Only the thought of being easily found out had stopped him. But now there was no question of being found out, because Jasper did not exist to anyone else.

Roderick stood up and moved clear of the desk so that

he could have an unimpeded run at his brother, ensuring that the full force of his stocky shoulders would be brought to bear.

"I do not know whether you have come here of your own accord or whether I have brought you back myself," said Roderick. "I cannot seem to repel you by thought alone. So I will dispatch you as I should have done to start with."

And then he took four sharp, running steps and crashed with his bunched right shoulder into the apparition of his brother standing there. But there was no shock of body on body, no shattering glass or splintered window frame. Roderick staggered, missed crashing through the window himself by a hair's-breadth, fell to the floor, got up immediately and looked round the room.

Jasper was gone.

Involuntarily, Roderick went to the window to look out. Below him on the pavement stood Jasper looking up at him and still smiling. Roderick stared fiercely down at him, Jasper seemed to lift an arm as if in farewell, turned and walked past the black-sailed ships tied up at the quay – just as he had always done. Roderick's eyes followed him as he walked further away, receding into the distance and finally out of sight – almost as if he was setting out into the world to assume an independent existence.

Now began for Roderick a strange time. At first he felt free: he exulted in what he had done. To get rid of a brother once was grand: twice was miraculous. But the other half of his bargain with himself was not easy. To start with, he assumed he was rid of the need to fear water as well. But the next day he walked across to the quayside and watched the oily swell below him licking darkly at worn brickwork, felt sick and retired to think again. No, the fear would not go. He was stuck with his vow.

A prisoner still, he could not concentrate on his work. Day after day he sat at the desk while letters, telegrams, bills and orders piled up. His eyes were held by the window: he could not tear them away. Independent of

125

him, they were waiting for a golden light, a shadowy shape, to reappear. But nothing ever did. Even in his dreams he waited. He dreamt he was waiting night after night after night, for a face which never appeared.

For months the Blackhull Line ran of its own accord. It took a long time for Roderick's new inertia to have an effect. But soon he realized something must be done. As he walked each day into the office ever more dirty, ragged and unkempt, even he realized how strangely the clerks regarded him. As he looked at the desk piled high with unanswered mail even he realized that the Blackhull Line would be ruined if someone did not take control. But who? He knew well now he was quite unable to.

The shipping world was not surprised when Roderick Blackhull announced he was selling the Blackhull Line to the highest bidder. Strange stories about him had been circulating for some time. There was no shortage of buyers and when Roderick left the office for the last time he was a very rich man indeed – rich enough, he thought, to insulate himself entirely from the fears which still kept leaking into his mind.

He retired completely from public life: in fact he was virtually never seen by anybody at all. He lived like a hermit, a recluse, in darkened rooms, behind locked doors. At all costs he kept up his resolve to stay away from water: had any of his old acquaintances been able to see him they would have been shocked at the sight of this hairy man, with a skin like putty through lack of light and sun, shuffling round his untidy domain. He kept his staff of servants on, paying them well and ordering them not to talk to anyone outside. But they were only human after all, and the strange tales about Roderick Blackhull were soon added to.

Roderick eventually realized that without fail he must move away from the sea. Its pressure so near oppressed him: its sullen roar filled him with dread. He bought a house inland and stayed there for six months. His fears disappeared – then slowly they returned. The waiting in his dreams changed: he felt the one awaited would soon arrive. Then came an urge to move on and escape his pursuers. He bought another house far away: the same happened. He bought another; soon he possessed four large homes, one in Worcestershire, one in Yorkshire, one in Norfolk, one in Cornwall. All were well inland: all gave him temporary peace. But after six months in each home, the dreams started again. The familiar rippling face appeared and the voice sounded. "You *will* die by water. I shall wait for you. The time comes nearer every day."

Whenever that dream came, then next morning a special train would be ordered. In front, a luggage van would be packed with such belongings as Roderick needed for his nomadic life. Second was a saloon and sleeping car combined, in which the curtains were drawn and the doors locked. At the rear were two ordinary passenger coaches in which the staff ate and slept as best they could – because the train would be loaded by day and always by night would it steam slowly from refuge to refuge, like a Flying Dutchman of the rails.

Eventually, the cycle was complete and established. In a great clockwise sweep Roderick Blackhull's strange caravan traversed the country: from the half timbered glebe house set in soft orchards in Worcestershire to the grey, solid domain, bought from a mill-owner, on the edge of the Yorkshire Moors; then south east through Lincolnshire to the warm red-brick dwelling on high ground in the Breckland; then west, skirting London and bowling down the Great Western Railway to the stone pile near Truro where people were few, the solitude complete and the sea kept properly at bay below granite cliffs several miles away.

Four times the circle was traced: half a year in each house, then move on because the underwater face was bubbling out its message yet again. Nine years had passed when suddenly the dreams changed. The face was saying something else.

"Nearly time, Roderick. Nearly time. As you laid in wait for me, so I will for you. Death by water, Roderick."

This time, Roderick woke convulsively. He looked round him. It was daylight already. A weak East Anglian sun tried to filter in round the edges of his thick curtains. He jumped out of bed and shouted for his manservant.

The following afternoon, the special train steamed on its journey westwards.

Roderick's train would come to its final halt at Truro: a panting tank engine would bring its load to a gaslit bay platform in the dark small hours of the morning and the train would stand quiet till day broke, Roderick woke and horsedrawn carts would take him and his belongings four miles inland to his home for the next half-year. That was the plan.

The sun had gone in after the train passed Taunton in the early evening. Clouds descended with the dark: the wind rose and rains squalls scudded against the carriage windows. A midnight storm raged as the train felt its way across the Royal Albert Bridge and entered the Duchy of Cornwall. The journey was nearly over. Roderick in his soft wheelborne bed slept soundly and so far dreamlessly.

Ten miles up the line from Truro the rails divided. The main line bore west, for Truro and Penzance. A branch line crept insignificantly south: within a quarter of a mile it crossed the river Fowey where it was still tidal. To let china-clay boats get upstream, the railway crossed by means of a swing bridge: a whole section of line could swing out to right angles and let ships pass on either side. Then it swung back and the trains could cross. There were few boats and fewer trains, so the great iron wheel in the junction signal box which when turned, opened and shut the bridge, was seldom used.

Two miles away, in the ticket office of a tiny station, before a roaring fire and listening to the now crashing storm outside, the stationmaster and the relief signalman sat with mugs of tea and discussed the signalman who was at that moment on duty in the junction box.

This man had not been there very long. He had, it seemed, been transferred from another district of the railway; he spoke to no one; he appeared for his working shifts and went home no one knew where. Was he married? Did he have children? His workmates had no idea. And, truth to tell, they did not care overmuch. "So what if he be a funny old fellow? Cornwall's a funny old place," was all they said.

So perhaps it was the flickering shadows made by the fire and the gaslight that caused the stationmaster to mention the new arrival – the funny old shadows cast on the wall.

"Have he ever spoke to you?" said the stationmaster.

"Why me? Why should he speak to me above others?"

"You work with him. You share the box with him. He be your mate."

"He's no mate of mine."

They drank their scalding tea deeply and reflectively. The gas flares flickered: the huge kettle on the fire sang quietly to itself.

The relief signalman continued.

"He's no mate of mine. He don't speak to me because I don't speak to him."

"But you work with him," replied the stationmaster.

"He chills me," was the reply. "He gives a chill in my stomach and to my heart when I see him."

"Aye," murmured the other. "That he does to me as well."

"Where he goes there is a silence around him. No birds sing when he is there. When I walk up the line to the box I can see him in there for a hundred yards or more, with the sun shining through the glass panes behind him. There he is standing, with the sun behind him, one of his hands on the swing bridge wheel. Just standing there, waiting for me. And I climb the steps and I call out to him but he never answers. He just stands there, with the sun shining on his fair head. Then he seems to come alive, and he signs the book and off he goes. And that's him gone till next shift."

"Ah," said the stationmaster. "He signs the book when he goes off duty. How does he sign it?"

"Danged if I can read it. 'Tis a scrawl I can't make head nor tail of."

Again, there was the companionable silence. The firelight and the gas flare chased shadows round the walls, helped by the high wind outside which crept in through the wooden window frames. The stationmaster watched them, and watched also where the gas flare and the fire together made different shadows. He saw that from his chair there was a black shadow caused by the fire which stretched from beside him away into the centre of the room and a lighter shadow from the gas flare that inched its way weakly behind him. And that a parallel black shadow crossed the room from his companion, while a weak shadow from the gas flare tried in vain to reach him. Watching these shadows, how they moved and swayed in the half-light, made him give voice to a speculation which surprised him even as he said it.

"You and I in here," he said, "we have two shadows. How many do you suppose our friend would have?"

"Why, if he were to come in here and sit between us, then he would have two the same as us."

"Would he?"

"But he never would come in here to sit between us."

"And if he did," said the stationmaster, his voice rising, "would he cast a shadow? Think on it, man. You know him better than I do."

And the relief signalman thought. And he remembered the still, waiting shape with sunlight reflected off its hair, he remembered how he clumped noisily up the wooden stairs to the signal box but the man he replaced seemed to drift down without sound, how there was never word between them, how – and here he caught his breath – no matter how bright the sun shone in and how golden was

130

the reflected light of the man's hair, there was no shadow, without a trace of a doubt there was no shadow from him to cross the floor, as there would be from anybody else in the whole world.

So he could do no more than whisper, "The man casts no shadow."

There was a roaring away along the line; the night train for Plymouth and London clattered through, leaving drifts of steam inside the little room.

"By God, but there are strange things that happen in this old Cornwall," said the stationmaster.

The relief found his voice properly.

"So what have we got in charge of the junction signal box?" he said.

The two men looked at each other.

"Come on," said the stationmaster.

They struggled into boots and oilskins, seized lanterns, put out the gas and rushed outside, to be met by the buffeting wind and stinging rain on their faces.

As they forced their way against the gale, they had no idea of what they might find. Why should they find anything? It was difficult to believe that a ghost would be recruited to man a signal box on the Great Western Railway. Even so, something in their hearts pushed them on as hard as they could go.

The squally gale stung their faces even more as they struggled on in the darkness – as if something in the elements was physically pushing them back. Their boots scrunched in the stone ballast between the rails, slipped on the wet, black wooden sleepers or grazed along the cinder six-foot way. Their lanterns, one white to show the way, the other shaded red to warn, hardly penetrated the blackness. The men were out of breath, panting from deep down in their lungs, almost falling over with the effort to keep on. But they kept on all the same, because the unknown impelled them.

They had stumbled along for all but a quarter of a mile.

Their faces were numb with wind and rain. They had passed two signals on the way, a distant and a home, both set to red. But now they were aware that the wires running by the track which connected the signals to the levers in the box had moved. Both signals had been set to green: the way was clear to a train approaching behind them.

"Ghost or not, he can pull them levers," shouted the stationmaster over the storm.

The men were now running in between the banks of a cutting, so the wind was a little less strong on them. The line curved here: the banks hid what was round the bend. But soon they could see the signal box, the lights inside glowing behind the windows.

"There he be," cried the relief man.

There indeed stood the signalman, plainly silhouetted in the light through the window.

"Like always," continued the relief. "Look at him – there like a statue, as if he's waiting, one hand on the swing bridge wheel."

They had two hundred yards still to run. Suddenly, above the wind, they were aware that the signalled train was following them fast – a humming from the rails, then a shrill whistle and the first sounds of the exhaust beat of a steam engine being smartly worked up a slight gradient.

The men were nearly there. Above them loomed the signal box: the signalman inside was now very clear to be seen, looking down on them gravely.

"He's there," shouted the stationmaster. "Up the steps, quick."

They clattered up the wooden stairway to the door. The stationmaster turned the handle. It did not budge.

"He's locked it," he muttered.

"Oh, God, look what he's doing," shouted the relief.

The signalman had leant to one lever and heaved back on it. Now he turned to the great iron wheel which worked the swing bridge and turned it easily clockwise.

"He's set the points for the branch line and opened the swing bridge," shrieked the relief. "He'll wreck the train."

132

The stationmaster smashed the glass panel in the door with the lamp – but even as he did so, there was no need, for suddenly the door swung easily. The relief sprang inside the box and heaved on the wheel. It was stuck immoveably. Grunting with strain he yet managed to call to the stationmaster.

"Get outside with the red lamp. Try to stop that train."

The stationmaster hurled himself down the steps and ran desperately along the track, waving the red lamp and shouting hoarsely against the wind.

A sudden and unexpected glare of sheet lightning – the first of the night – lit up the land. In its two-second glow the oncoming train could be seen – a tank engine, a luggage van and three coaches – steaming on confidently and unsuspectingly.

"Come and help me, can't you?" screamed the relief as he hung on to the unmoving wheel. No one came to his aid. He stole a look round the box as he heaved.

It was empty.

Now the train was passing: its roar, with the door open, was deafening. He caught a glimpse of the driver and fireman on the footplate, lit by the orange glow of the fire. They were both standing up and looking forward, their heads stuck out over the cab side. Surely they could see the red lamp. Then the coaches clattered past. In another second, the signal box was filled with white, sulphur-smelling steam as the exhaust from the engine's chimney drifted in through the open door and for a moment there was a damp fog.

During that moment, the relief heard the squealing, metallic roar of brakes being applied – too late, surely, at that speed. And when the steam cleared, he saw something else.

The signalman was there after all. He stood in the far corner of the signal box, his arms folded, his lips smiling, his fair hair oddly shining in the lamplight.

The relief stared at him speechlessly.

133

Clumping steps made him realize the stationmaster had returned.

"She's gone past," gasped the stationmaster. "Took the points at forty miles an hour: nearly derailed herself going on to the branch. They saw me and put their brakes on. But they'll never stop in time."

He, too, saw the standing, smiling signalman. He lunged towards him.

"What are you doing?" he shouted.

The signalman spoke,

"Death by water," he said. "For one man. No one else will be harmed. For one man only. Death by water, as I promised."

And he vanished.

The smell of sulphur hung even more heavily as the sky was lit up by a second burst of sheet lightning.

The sound of screaming brakes had continued all the time, getting gradually further away. Abruptly they stopped. Then, above the noise of the wind and the beating raindrops on the window, there was a confused hissing roar which ended as suddenly as it started. The two men alone in the singal box looked at each other with surmising horror.

Roderick Blackhull was still sleeping soundly. However, he was now dreaming – a dream which was gaining every second in piercing intensity.

Jasper was there again – as ever, rippling under clear water, fair hair rising and falling.

"The time has come, brother. At long last the time has come."

Roderick found himself able to talk.

"That is impossible," he said. "I have rid myself of you and I have rid myself of water. So you can be no more than a dream."

"No, brother, no," said Jasper. "There is no escape for you. Join me here where it is cool and clean, and clear, so our funeral barge can take us far into eternity with the dignity our deaths on earth cannot provide."

134

Suddenly, to Roderick it was very tempting. To be rid of the pursuit, to bow to inevitability, to admit that his crime had brought nothing but misery and fear and to make – at last – amends; these things were all at once so beautiful that he could not resist them.

In his dream he bent down, lower and lower towards Jasper. He felt the cool water rise as he took his place beside his brother. He lay back and opened his mouth to take great gulps of the sweet, clear liquid. But he gasped with shock because it was salty, murky and choking: it was filthy and bitterly cold: it cut out all light and all sound, suffocating him till his lungs burst and oblivion succeeded the quiet laughter of his brother.

It was seen as miraculous that in such a terrible disaster only one person was killed. In evidence afterwards, the driver and fireman told how when they saw in the lightning burst the swing bridge standing open, the rails ahead coming to an abrupt end, they both without thinking jumped, only suffering cuts and bruises. The train was slowing all the time – even so, they looked with horror as the driverless engine teetered on the brink and fell into the river, followed by the luggage van and the saloon-cum-sleeping car. Then – and this they saw as the work of Providence – the couplings between the saloon and the rear coaches snapped: the two coaches stayed on the rails. No one inside was hurt.

The survivors huddled in the storm looking down at the swirling river into which a locomotive, a van, a coach and one man had disappeared.

Next day, cranes brought the saloon coach to the surface. Inside was found the sole occupant; Mr Roderick Blackhull, the well-known shipping magnate. He was drowned: trapped in his little bedroom cubicle with no chance of escape – the very last place, everybody agreed, where one might expect to meet death by water.

The stationmaster and relief were congratulated for their promptness in trying to save the train: their ludicrous story about ghostly signalmen who vanished into thin air was discounted as being an impression induced by the urgency of the situation. It was assumed that the miscreant had made good his escape while the other two men were occupied. The police were called upon urgently to find him and bring him to trial.

But he was never found.

On that terrible night, the storm had raged for hours after the train had fallen into the River Fowey. Many people, unable to sleep, had several times looked through curtains and shutters out to the river and the sea beyond, as the lightning palely burst, fearful for the safety of those out of sight of land. And next day, they agreed on one thing. They had seen a ship unfamiliar to them: a barquentine which sailed down the river and out to sea, steadily and smoothly, despite the angry wind and water. Though such a wind called for as little canvas as possible, the ship bore a full press of sails. No one had seen her enter harbour: everyone was surprised that so large a ship could have come from so far up river.

And as they watched her progress through the harbour and out to sea, to disappear into the inky vastness beyond, every one of them was quite sure – each time the lightning lit up the air round her – of one thing.

Her sails were all jet black.

The Shirt Off a
Hanged Man's Back

*What terrible thing has happened? As I run, my mind is full
of anguish. Air fills the lungs of my hard fit body and the
shouts of the angry crowd behind me die away as I
outdistance them. My strong legs drive me on.*

But who will hear me?

*My fists still clenched, I run on alone. My shirt flaps
behind me: I have knotted the arms round my waist so the
air still cools my bare, sweating shoulders.*

My mind is in turmoil. I know my journey soon will end.

But who will hear me?

*In all time stretched out before me, who will hear me?
My horror and my terror are so great that they reach out of
my own age to whoever can hear me.*

Joanna was cold. So was Steve. The clear mid-May night
sky still bore a hint of winter frosts.

And it was so dark. There was no moon. The high
hedge and the higher trees on each side of the narrow road
kept out what light came from the stars. They hemmed
Joanna and Steve in. Just as well. There was no need to
think about the wide, hedgeless, featureless expanse
which stretched away on either side.

They walked arm-in-arm, Steve on the right, Joanna on
the left. Steve shone his torch ahead, waving it around so
its thin, wild light gave no direction, only a little comfort.

Joanna spoke, more to hear her own voice than to say
anything worthwhile.

"It was a good disco."

Steve didn't answer.

It was a two-mile walk from the village to Crossways

Farm where Joanna lived and Scratch Cottages where Steve lived with his grandmother, on the very edge of the sloping, concave green of Harrow's Common. So when the weekly disco ended, because there was no one to take them back to their lonely homes, the two were faced with the long trek back together for no other reason than they lived so close. They had become used to the quiet, companionable amble along what was once the old coaching road from London to Cambridge – so much so that the cold never chilled them, the darkness never oppressed them, the loneliness never frightened them.

Until tonight.

Why tonight?

Because there was something in the air; something indefinable; something fearful. Both felt it; neither said anything about it. But they were both watchful.

The thin beam from Steve's torch cut inconsequential white lines in the darkness. He shone it on the road ahead, on the grass verges, up in the trees. And then Joanna screamed; her fingers dug into Steve's arm so that the pain even through the cloth of his coat made him wince.

"What did you do that for?" he demanded.

"There's a body hanging from the tree," Joanna gasped.

"Don't be daft," said Steve.

He shone the torch wildly round. Then he too caught his breath.

Ten feet above their heads, hanging from a branch, was what seemed to be a limp, white body swaying loosely to and fro, its thin arms waving independently.

"It's someone dead," Joanna managed to say.

Steve continued to wave his torch.

"Don't look. It's horrible," urged Joanna.

"I don't believe it," said Steve.

"It's there, in front of your eyes," said Joanna.

Steve laughed suddenly and picked up a stone.

"I'll see how dead it is," he said.

138

He threw the stone with his right hand while he aimed the torch at the hanging shape with his left. The stone hit the shape and seemed to go through it without hindrance.

Joanna was mystified. Steve shone his torch directly on it. He laughed again.

"It's an old shirt," he said.

And it was. A dirty old white shirt, strangely long like an ancient nightshirt, hanging from a main branch of a horse chestnut tree, waving in the slight breeze like a limp, formless body.

Now Joanna could laugh herself.

"Fancy being scared of that," she said.

The feeling of relief was tremendous. The fright was over.

So you have seen the sign my enemies left. It was to be a warning. Instead, it will bring you to me.

So be it. There will be spectators for this last act. I will make them watch.

I will make them watch because already I know what will happen to me. I have done a terrible thing and did not mean it. And I am a stranger here: those who seek me are not of my kin and things will not fall out well for me.

I will make these two – whoever they are, whenever they live – understand. I am not in my own land and they will see that what is right is done for me. For no one else will. No one here can act for me.

I am alone.

The fright was over.

Or was it?

They walked another quarter of a mile.

"I still feel scared," said Joanna.

Yes. There was still something in the air. Ahead of them was a movement. They stopped and strained their eyes forward. Someone was coming to meet them. Someone running.

"A jogger," said Steve. "He's out late. Must have been a few miles."

It was a man. He wore dark, narrow trousers – more like tights. A lighter-coloured sash was tied round his waist. His chest was bare; in the torchlight they could see sweat glistening on his body.

"Your shirt's down the road, mate," called Steve. "You'll have to climb the tree to get it."

The running man turned his head and looked at them; Joanna knew she would never forget the face she then saw. For the awful churning fear she had felt when she first saw the shirt had returned worse than before.

Steve shone the torch after the man.

"He must have picked up speed a bit. Or he's in the hedge. He's disappeared."

Joanna looked at Steve. She knew he felt the same as she did. They started running and didn't stop until they were safe in their own homes.

See? My story will unfold before you.

Already you are seeking me, though you do not know it. Soon you will know who I am and why I am here. And why I need you.

Come with me now.

Joanna slept badly that night. She kept seeing the face of the running man. It was not an attractive face. Framed by lank, black hair, it was firm, angry, sad and fearful all at once and also misshapen. There was a swollen puffiness about it – as if the owner had been in a fight. She was sure there was blood on it. When the face faded, another strong impression took its place. She seemed to be part of a great shouting, baying crowd – a huge press of men pushing forward and yelling in ugly voices, roaring encouragement and abuse, striving to see something hidden from her which was violent and raised strong passions.

In the small hours of the morning she woke. The room was deathly quiet. She got out of bed and drew the curtain to look out of her window. The moon was now up in a

140

clear sky. In front of her were her father's fields and the narrow road that formed the approach to Crossways Farm. Further away she could see where a cart-track crossed that private road. The road looked different somehow – more like a track. Oddly, the cart-track looked more like a road. And where they met she saw something unfamiliar. At first it looked like a cross, perhaps marking a grave. She looked again and realized it was not a cross. It was a wooden signpost. A dark figure stood by it, looking up as if trying to make the words out on the signpost arms.

She went back to bed and was soon asleep again. Next morning, when she remembered the sight, she thought she must have dreamt it.

By ten o'clock, she began to wonder. The day was bright and clear with a stiffer breeze than the one which made the shirt wave the night before. So the person standing at the junction of driveway and cart-track just where the figure of the night before had been was easy to recognize.

"I had a dream last night," Steve said when Joanna went out to see what he was doing there. "It must have been a dream. But it didn't half seem real."

"What was it?" said Joanna.

"I was here. Standing here, on this spot. Wind on my face; grass under my feet. It was real. But it was all different."

"How?"

"This road wasn't tarred over for a start. And your farmhouse was there but your outbuildings were all different. But that wasn't the biggest change."

"I know," said Joanna.

"What do you mean?"

"Was there a signpost here?"

"Yes. How did you know?"

So it wasn't a dream.

"I saw you," said Joanna. "You were standing by it and looking up, like you were trying to make out what was written on it."

141

"What do you mean, you saw me? I was dreaming."

"Then why have you come to see if the signpost is still here?"

Steve ignored the question.

"I'd come there to wait for someone," he said. "But he never turned up."

"Who?"

"I don't know. I waited for hours under the signpost and then went home. Next I knew, I'd woken up this morning."

A thought formed in Joanna's mind.

"You haven't seen the jogger again, have you?"

"No. Nor his shirt."

"I have," said Joanna.

"Let me get this straight," said Steve. "I dream I go along to wait for someone I don't know somewhere on your farm. There's a signpost there that's not here now. It's such a real dream it's like I'm really there. Nobody turns up. But you're watching me. I don't get it."

"I thought I dreamt seeing you through the window. But I couldn't have been if you were really there."

Steve spoke with finality.

"Where were your outbuildings last night? What happened to the road surfaces? Where did the signpost come from? Why were all the hedges and trees different?" His voice was insistent.

"How should I know?" said Joanna.

"Last night when I was out there, it was back in the past. I don't know how far back. Years and years.

Joanna said nothing.

"There's no other way to explain it. Either we had exactly the same dream or we were really there."

"Why should it happen to us?" Joanna said.

I fix all my thoughts on you. Listen to me. Look at me. You can see me if you try. You have seen me before: I brought you here once. Come here again. Stay with me. Watch, so you know what to do.

142

The wounds on my face are smarting and throbbing. My fists are sore and bleeding. Would that I could cut them off. "If your right hand offends you, cut it off." Our Lord and Saviour told us that: how I wish I could obey him. My right hand offends me because of what it has done.

And still I run and even my great lungs begin to fail me. Turn now and look at me.

Joanna did not see the face in her dreams that night. But she did not know what made her wake up at the same time as the previous night.

There was the same deathly quiet. Once again the moon was up and through the window she could see the countryside bathed in its washed-out, grey light.

The signpost was there. Nobody stood by it. Joanna hesitated a moment – then pulled her clothes on quickly and went downstairs through the sleeping house and out into the fresh night air.

The steady breeze was cold on her face as she walked. When she had left the house behind she turned and looked back.

Everything looked changed. Her home, the old farmhouse, was recognizable. But where were the cowsheds, the Dutch Barn? There was a jumble of tumbledown buildings she had never seen before. And where was the roadway she knew so well, tarred and paved and well able to bear a Land-Rover or a tractor? Here was merely a rutted track of beaten earth and stones fit only for carts. Steve had been right.

She hastened to the signpost. The idea was forming in her mind that she, like Steve, was there to wait for someone, though she had no idea who.

She looked up at the arms of the signpost. Pointing up and down the way she had come were the words LONDON and CAMBRIDGE. The track which crossed it led to the two nearest villages.

Footsteps sounded beside her. She turned quickly. Steve was approaching.

"There you are," she said to him. "It wasn't a dream."

"How do you know?" he said. "I might be in your dream. Or you in mine."

Joanna looked around her again.

"But what's happened?" she said.

Steve didn't answer. He was looking down the track behind her. She turned and followed his gaze. The silent, running figure was approaching them again. Was this who they had come here to wait for?

He drew level with them and once again slowly turned his face. The same damaged face, puffy, misshapen, bloodstained. His chest still ran with sweat. In the moonlight they could see better what he was wearing; not tights but narrow knee breeches and stockings below them.

"It's him again," said Steve.

The man beckoned.

"He wants us to follow," said Joanna.

The man ran on. Joanna and Steve stumbled after him. He was leading them back along the way they had come from the disco when they had first seen the shirt. But all was different; the hedges and trees were smaller and thinner; the road was still just a track. And still the man ran, evenly, with no change in pace or slackening of stride. And Steve and Joanna struggled to keep him in sight.

He stopped. The two slowed down and approached him warily. He was standing under a horse chestnut tree and pointed upwards.

"Look," breathed Joanna.

Hanging from a branch ten feet up was the shirt.

Exactly the same as before; long, white, limp, with crazily flapping arms. The two looked at it in complete puzzlement, while the man stood still, mute, pointing upwards.

"Listen," said Steve.

Now they heard the first noise that had come to their ears besides their own voices. A confused and ugly roar;

144

shouts, yells, a betokening of extreme anger. It was the noise of a mob on the march. They turned to where it came from, expecting to see hundreds of people. But though the noise was unbearable in their ears, not a soul was to be seen.

They looked back to the man for explanation.

He was not there.

They looked up at the shirt.

And Joanna let out a louder scream than that which had greeted her first sight of it. For the man was now wearing it. And he was hanging from the branch; dangling limply to and fro, giving human form to the shape of the shirt.

Now you have seen. Now you know what is to happen. Now you can stay with me throughout my travail. Oh, my children, now you know my fate, I can speak to you directly. There are so many years between us; so many years for me to have waited till I can be freed. Now I can show you.

Watch. You must watch.

Before Joanna could take the sight in, she heard a voice. A low voice, a lilting brogue, talking quickly. She and Steve turned round. But nobody was there: the voice was all around them, echoing – yet as well somehow in their own heads, speaking urgently to both of them.

"At last I can talk to you. Seen me you have already and followed me you have at last and met me only when you saw what fell to me at the end before the mob comes to cut my body down. Seen me and met me you have, to put right the great wrong done to me."

"Why us?" said Steve.

"You will see."

"Who are you?" said Joanna.

"Who am I? I am Lanahan. I am the fighting Irish Paddy, the pride of County Galway, the champion of the Emerald Isle, the scourge of the English bully-boys. The bare-fisted king of the milling fraternity. As Pierce Egan would say. Him you will soon see."

145

"A prize-fighter," said Steve. "An old-fashioned boxer. I've read about them."

"You will know more soon. You, boy, especially. It is in your blood."

The voice lilted on, disembodied but deep in their ears. As it spoke, they were aware that the hanging figure in front of them disappeared and the tree it dangled from with it. The scene dissolved around them, reformed and was at once known to them.

"Harrow's Common," breathed Joanna.

Yes, Harrow's Common it was, just as they always knew it, bathed in afternoon sunlight. Except that in the middle was something quite new: two roped-off squares, one inside the other. The one inside was fully thirty feet square; the outer a good fifty. The grass in the inner ring was whitened with sawdust.

"See," said the lilting voice of Lanahan. "The field of glory."

They looked beyond the ring. And now they saw the crowds approaching. People in their hundreds drew near. Broughams, post chaises and larger carriages were driven up and the horses, when they stopped, chewed unconcerned at the grass. Men in exquisitely cut and coloured coats and breeches picked their way finickily across the rough grass to the outer ring.

"Look at them," said the voice of Lanahan. "The Fancy. Both the Lords and the flash gents. The rich amateurs. Those for whose money we fight. One of them is Lord Fawkon. My patron. I am no more than his creature. Also there is Colonel Waddis; he will keep the time. And Captain Scattergood, the gallant umpire. For such good men how can I fail to fight myself to a standstill?" The voice now had a sharp edge of sarcasm to it.

As the voice spoke, Joanna and Steve saw the faces of the Fancy; well-fed, supercilious features – aquiline noses and sharp chins. Or reddened, roughened, flabby jowls and drooping rolls of fat around the neck. Joanna

146

remembered the face of Lanahan she had already seen and thought of the anguish it showed beside the unconcern of these.

And more men came. Rough men, poor men, shouting and jostling men. Hundreds of men, fighting for good positions round the ring.

The voice spoke again.

"We have come to Harrow's Common. Today, I fight the young hopeful, James Phipps. I am champion of Ireland. Lord Fawkon brought me here from Ireland to fight. I beat Cobb in half an hour, battering him till he could neither see nor stand. I hammered Driver till his face was like a joint of beef and he gave in. So now I am the darling of the Fancy. Soon I might fight Daniel Mendoza or the great Tom Cribb. But now the stripling James Phipps has challenged me on his own ground and I cannot refuse. Three times before we have tried to fight; each time the magistrates have got wind of it and now we are driven over the boundary to another shire. But here all is well; the Lord Lieutenant will not stop us from breaking the law. He is one of the Fancy himself and has placed his bet on Phipps the local boy. Last night I was brought by my backers to the Bull at Royston as my headquarters for the fight; young Phipps left his village down the road to lodge at the Wheatsheaf in Barkway. So now the sun shines on Harrow's Common, the ring is set up, sawdust is spread over the turf. My colours of green and his of blue are twined together at the stake. And see, Pierce Egan the commentator, the recorder for the sporting papers, has come; the man who never misses a fight of note and who writes down all that happens for those who can read it. Egan is here, so my fight will not be forgotten.

They saw a man leaning on a post of the inner ring; a gaudy figure in a red coat and wearing a tall stovepipe hat. Egan the sporting journalist.

The noisy crowd was stilled; every eye turned to the ring. The field of glory was yet empty. The voice went on.

"Look, my fists are pickled with brine, my seconds and bottleholder are behind me and into the ring on the other side comes Phipps. James Phipps, for whom I have only friendship but must now try to beat into insensibility."

The man they knew as Lanahan they could now see, ducking through the ropes of the inner ring. A younger man had entered on the opposite side. Both were accompanied by their seconds and bottleholders. The dark, chunky figure faced the boyish one. The younger man spoke. Both Joanna and Steve could hear the words plainly.

"I hope you are well, Lanahan."

"Very well, my boy," said Lanahan. "And soon we will be talking to each other in another language."

"Aye," said Phipps. His voice had an East Anglian burr Joanna and Steve knew well. "Our fists will raise a fine crop of red flowers on our faces sure enough."

"By all the saints, young Jim," said Lanahan. "One of us will have his eyes closed by nightfall and sorry I am indeed that it will be you."

"How they talk," said Joanna to Steve and turned to him when he did not answer. Steve's eyes were fixed in wonder at the sight of Phipps.

"Look at him," he said. "*It's me.*"

Joanna looked. Yes, it was. The same curly, dark red hair and cheerful round features.

"It's me," said Steve again. "Phipps is a relation. He's in my family about two hundred years back."

He looked eagerly at the ring.

"Come on Jim," he shouted. "Give the Mick what for."

"But Steve," said Joanna. "We're here to help Lanahan. That's why he's brought us back."

"That could be my brother in the ring," said Steve. He shouted again. "Come on, Jim. Bash his teeth in."

"Nobody can hear you," said Joanna.

The Irish voice, like a disembodied commentator, sounded again.

"So you see why I have waited for you all these centuries. Yes, he is your kinsman. So only you can help me."

148

"What about me?" said Joanna.

"You will understand," said the voice.

Both men had left the ring, each to a barouche drawn up some way outside it. The buzz of conversation among the crowd of men sitting and standing on the grass and leaning out of the carts, chaises and other horse-drawn vehicles ringing the arena died. The two men, now stripped to the waist for action, appeared. Then the cheering burst out again: encouragement shouted in words curious to Joanna's and Steve's ears.

"Go it, Jim. Tap the Paddy's claret."

Lanahan had few friends here.

Captain Scattergood, from his umpire's position outside the ring, called the men to come up to the scratch. And they did, facing each other, in the exact middle of the ring, squaring up to each other in oddly stiff, stilted attitudes. The clenched fists, looking like legs of lamb, were held in front of their faces. For a moment they stood, making no move, sizing each other up, perfectly poised, with advantage to neither.

The fight was on.

Pierce Egan, the man with the stovepipe hat, leaned forward on to the ropes of the inner ring, taking in every detail.

"Do you see him?" said the voice of Lanahan. "Do you see Mr Egan? He's the man for the writing down of it all. Every word he said of the fight I can tell you by heart. Except the very last."

The men in the ring began to move at last, warily, watchfully.

"Listen to Egan," said the voice. "Here are his words. 'First round. Several feints took place, but PHIPPS, not minding his distance, hit short. *Lanahan* took advantage of the fault and put in a severe blow to PHIPPS'S throat and PHIPPS was levelled.'"

The young man was sprawled on the ground. Lanahan blew on his fists and walked back to his corner, Phipps's second hustled him back to the opposite corner.

"I have the measure of him already," said Lanahan's voice. "It was a foolish man who pitted him against me. But the half-minute is up and we must to the scratch again. Let Egan speak.

"'Second Round. PHIPPS distressed already – *Lanahan bang up*, flourishing with all the graces of the science and showing himself to be the prime. PHIPPS full of game. *Lanahan* gave a severe blow upon the ear, causing PHIPPS'S blood to flow. PHIPPS rallied with a severe hit up on *Lanahan's* breast, but *Lanahan* brought him down with a terrible blow to the nose and the claret flowed freely.'

"It is happening again. Throughout all the years I have seen it over and over again: it will not leave me. Just once, just once, could it be different? No, it is useless to think it. From now, the end is inevitable. So listen to Egan.

"'Round three. PHIPPS came up to the scratch greatly distressed. *Lanahan* took advantage with several severe blows. Now for gameness and pluck, PHIPPS showed up to his best. In warding off *Lanahan's* most ferocious hits, he showed he was not without science. But a real facer from *Lanahan* knocked all the breath out of his body.'"

For the first time, Steve spoke.

"This is terrible," he said. "That referee ought to stop it."

"Oh, Jesus, Mary mother of God and all the saints," cried the voice of Lanahan. "Why did young Jim keep coming back? Why do his seconds not throw in the towel?"

"'Fourth round. This was a truly bloody round – the hits were tremendous in the extreme. Notwithstanding his former hammering, PHIPPS stood up well in a fine display of their talents for milling. PHIPPS'S head was a frightful sight, like a side of beef, his left eye now being useless. *Lanahan* tripped and fell, thus ending the round. But though it was *Lanahan* who measured his length in the ring, yet evidently the round was once more in his favour. Odds fifteen-to-one on *Lanahan*.'

"I fell," groaned Lanahan's voice. "I fell and he thought he could still beat me. Oh Jim. Dear young Jim, do not come out for this round."

Steve was silent.

"'Round six to round nine. PHIPPS at first seemed in better spirits and *Lanahan* loudly praised the courage of his adversary but wished him to understand that he would be beaten. *Lanahan's* firmness was manifest and young PHIPPS'S features were rendered perfectly unintelligible: hardly a single feature could be traced. But the ENGLISHMAN, reluctant to pronounce the unpleasant sound of defeat, protracted the battle throughout these four rounds till exhaustion caused him to fall at the end of the ninth.'"

The crowd roared as Jim Phipp's seconds carried him back to the corner. Surely he could not come back again.

"Stop the fight. Stop the fight now. Do not bring him to the scratch again. Lose your money with a good grace," Lanahan's voice moaned.

But it was not to be. Phipps's seconds carried him to the centre of the ring, where he stood trying to raise his fists and then fell to the ground before Lanahan had even moved.

"You see?" said Lanahan's voice. "Just to give him more time for a rest. And this is all Egan can say: 'Round ten. Ended with PHIPPS on the floor and not a blow struck.'"

Steve spoke. "I know what's going to happen," he said.

"Listen to Egan," said Lanahan's voice. "'Round eleven. The fateful round. Now PHIPPS has not the smallest prospect of success but with great gameness and pluck he comes up to the scratch though oblivious of where he is. *Lanahan* said to him, "Give up now, James my boy, for I do not wish to hurt you further." But PHIPPS measures a light blow on *Lanahan's* ribs, whereupon Lanahan punishes him right and left to finish him till he falls insensible.'"

The blinded, bloodied, figure of James Phipps fell for

the last time to the ground. His second rushed in and carried him off. A towel fluttered to the centre of the ring from his corner. Lanahan had won. The silence was thunderous.

"Oh God," wailed the voice of *Lanahan*. "I know what I have done to him. The last blow I struck: I saw in his eyes as he fell what I had done. He will never rise again. I have killed him."

Joanna was shocked at Steve's voice. "You bastard," he shrieked. "He could have been my brother. You killed him."

"It's not his fault," said Joanna.

"He's killed my brother," shouted Steve.

"Steve," said Joanna. "This is two hundred years ago."

"He's a murderer. He killed my brother. He should hang for it."

Phipps was surrounded by a mob trying to see how damaged he was. Lanahan seemed alone in the ring, for a moment ignored. He turned, ducked under both sets of ropes and entered his barouche. Almost at once he emerged still stripped to the waist but with his white shirt flapping behind him and knotted by the sleeves round his waist. He walked away from the crowd, away from Harrow's Common, till he reached the road. Then he began to run: a steady, driving progress which took him down the road, towards Scratch Cottages and Crossways Farm, past the signpost and out towards the tree of the hanging.

Joanna and Steve, invisible to all else, had watched everything happen. As Lanahan disappeared from view, Joanna spoke.

"Well?" she said.

There were tears in Steve's eyes.

"He's killed Jim Phipps who was in my family. I feel like he killed my own brother. Why have I had to see this?"

"He wants you to forgive him," said Joanna.

"Forgive? I'm glad he's hanged. I'd have strung him up myself."

"But Steve, it's not Lanahan's fault. What could he do?"

"He could have stopped the fight himself if the referee wouldn't. He needn't have gone on."

"But shouldn't Phipps have given in earlier?"

"Why should he? If he thinks he's got a chance still, why should he?"

"But Steve, that doesn't add up. You can't have it both ways."

"I can and I will. Lanahan's a murderer and he deserves all he gets."

"Look behind you," said Joanna.

On Harrow's Common people were beginning to move. One or two pointed the way Lanahan had run. A knot of about fifty men, some of them the aristocratic members of the Fancy, some of them the flashy members of it, most of them roughly dressed, began to run after him. There was an ugly confused shouting: the noise Joanna had first heard as they saw Lanahan hanging. Murder was in their voices and their faces. Jim Phipps was now surely dead.

"Look at them," said Joanna. "They'd tear him to pieces if they caught him."

"So well they should," said Steve stubbornly.

The voice of Lanahan came again.

"No," it said. "They should not. But I feared they would. And yet I felt I deserved it. Come with me on my last run."

And they were there with him, hearing the retching gasps as he breathed, the remorseless plod of his feet on the rough road; seeing the sweat on his shoulders, the blood and bruises on his face. And somehow they could hear his thoughts.

What terrible thing has happened? As I run, my mind is full of anguish. Air fills the lungs of my hard fit body and the shouts of the angry crowd behind me die away as I outdistance them. My strong legs drive me on.

In all time stretched out before me, who will hear me? My horror and my terror are so great that they reach out of my own age to whoever can hear me.

I look through centuries and see no pity for me. Two

153

*figures stand by the road ahead. A boy and a girl. The boy
frightens me. It is Jim. Am I seeing Jim as he was? Or as his
nephew one day might be? For no help can I have from this
boy, no understanding at all when I have killed his kin. Yet
only from such as he can forgiveness come. And the girl.
There is both fear and compassion on her face. She will
understand. Perhaps she can make the kinsman of Jim
Phipps understand as well. In time I may be forgiven.*

"That you won't," said Steve out loud. "Not by me you
won't. You're running away now so you won't get what's
coming to you. But we've seen what's going to happen.
And you deserve it."

Lanahan reached the tree. He stopped and flopped
down on the grass beneath, exhausted. For a moment he
lay still, panting hard. Then he sat up, listening.

The baying shouts of the mob were getting closer.

Lanahan looked up the road and seemed to be starting
to run again. Then he must have thought better of it,
knowing he could not go much further. He untied the
sleeves of his shirt from round his waist and put it on, so it
flapped outside his breeches. He fastened the buttons up
to his chin. Then, slowly and awkwardly, he began to
climb the tree.

"You can't hide," shouted Steve. "They'll see you up
there. They'll have you down as soon as look at you."

"He can't hear you," said Joanna. "His ghost has called
us back to see all this but the man who's climbed the tree
is flesh and blood. He can't hear you."

Lanahan scrambled on to a branch about twenty feet up.
He sat on it, looking up the road to the approaching mob.

Once again, Joanna and Steve shared his thoughts.

*There is no escape for me. James Phipps's blood is on
my hands. In a land of strangers there is none to protect
me. If I go down to meet them, they'll kill me. If I stay here,
they will pull me down. If I try to run further, they will
catch me.*

Oh, James, James, why did you not give in? Your

bravery has cost you your young life. I would rather have lost my right hand than done what I have done. But your blood is on my soul. And there is no priest near me in this heretic land and I must die unshriven, unforgiven. Lord, have mercy upon me.

And what if I should end my life for myself? What if I should hurl myself from here to the hard ground beneath? Or if I should make a rope with my shirt to tie to the branch, with one end round my neck, to jump off and make a quick end of it? That way, I avoid the anger of my enemies.

But also I will be damned eternally. Two lives on my conscience. James Phipps's and my own. I shall be cast into the flames of hell for ever with two mortal sins scarring my soul and no one to give me the blessed sacraments. Mary, the mother of our Lord, help me.

Now the mob was well within sight.

"We see you, Lanahan. Come down, you Irish pig. Paddy the boy-killer."

Mary, mother of God and all you Saints, be with me now.

Instinctively, Lanahan began to climb higher. His bruised and bleeding hands suffered more as he gripped the rough bark of the tree. To the top was no escape: no miraculous ascension would take him away from his pursuers. He cast a look down. Angry, white faces far below. Abuse hurled up. His heart sank and waves of exhaustion engulfed him.

It is all up with me.

He pushed a weary right arm upwards to reach for a branch. A hard projecting stump, almost like a nail hammered into the trunk, tore into the sleeve of his shirt. He staggered with the sudden pain in his wrist and lost his footing. The stump ripped the cloth of his shirt. He fell. His fall lasted a few feet only. It was brought up short as the tearing of the cloth stopped at the hem of his cuff. The sudden shock checked his falling body and the gathered shirt met and pulled tight round his neck. It acted like a noose. Lanahan's life was over.

And Joanna saw the sight again which had before made her scream: the body hanging from the branch, dangling limply to and fro, giving human form to the shape of the shirt.

The crowd underneath was suddenly silent. Each man looked up, awed and perhaps guilty. A voice spoke.

"He's topped his bloody self."

There was a murmur of questioning voices. What were they to do now the body of their quarry hung above them?

A finely dressed man in a royal blue jacket, white breeches and a pink silk cravat stepped forward. He called for silence. It was granted at once as the crowd looked at him with deference. He spoke.

"Now then. You all – or most of you – know who I am. I am Lord Fawkon. I brought Lanahan to England to fight: I put up the stake money. He did as I bade him in life: now he will be treated in death the way I say."

There was a deferential murmur of acquiescence. Lord Fawkon continued.

"As you see, Lanahan has taken his own life. In doing so, he had put himself beyond all Christian help, even that of the Papist Church to which he belonged. We have to dispose of his body quickly for this affair must be kept quiet. If the magistrates hear of it, then the noble art of pugilism will not any more take place in this shire. Even my influence could not save it."

There was silence. Then a voice said, "So what do we do, my Lord?"

"A suicide," said Lord Fawkon, "is buried without funeral rites outside consecrated ground at a crossroads."

There was a roar of approval.

"There's a crossroads a mile back and more."

"Aye, at Crossways Farm."

"Bury him there under the signpost."

"Cut him down and we'll bear him along."

"Never," cried a loud voice from the back. "He killed our young Jim and deserved no burial. In the olden times

156

when the hanging judges swept the county for witches and rebels he'd have been left to swing and be eaten by the crows. And that's good enough for him."

Suddenly there was a conflict in the crowd. The last speaker had many to agree with him and for a moment it looked as if there might be a fight round about the tree. But Lord Fawkon raised his arm for silence and once again he received it.

"I know your feelings," he said, "and do in part share them. But Lanahan was a good man and a fine fighter and deserves better than that, no matter what we feel. He hanged himself with his shirt. Very well. Let us cut him down and bury him as we have said but also let us leave his shirt here, hanging from the branch on which he died. To those who do not know what has happened today, it will signify nothing . For those who do, it will have a meaning. It will be a memorial and a warning. And it will stay there until the elements rot it into nothingness."

Joanna and Steve took all this in as they watched. But now, as men climbed the tree to bring the body down and one tied the shirt to the branch so that it hung and flapped crazily in a way they both now knew so well, she collected her thoughts.

"Don't you see now why Lanahan called us back here?"

"No I don't," said Steve. "I wish I was with them there."

"They think he killed himself. But he didn't. Poor, innocent, misunderstood Lanahan. It was a terrible accident, even if it did put him out of his misery."

"Innocent? Him?" scoffed Steve.

"He's died unforgiven, buried like a suicide, damned for ever. Or so he thinks. and he's called us back as the only ones who can be his witnesses. He needs to be forgiven."

"I can't," said Steve.

The crowd bore the body back along the road. They reached the crossroads and the signpost. Then they ran for spades and mattocks. And Joanna remembered the night she came home from the disco and through her window saw the signpost in the moonlight. At first she thought it was a cross marking a grave. Now she knew that it was.

Men dug furiously. Joanna tried hard to memorise the exact position. Soon a trench five deep was at the foot of the signpost: Lanahan's body was placed in it. Then the grave was filled and most men left. A few stayed behind, standing awkwardly by with their hats off. Lord Fawkon, who had watched the burial from afar, came to the grave and stood silently for a few minutes. Then he walked to his carriage, which had been driven from Harrow's Common and had also stood waiting, the four horses champing reflectively. He boarded, the coachman set the horses going and the noble lord and his conveyance disappeared in a cloud of dust. The other men walked slowly away. The signpost stood deserted, a mound of freshly turned earth beneath it.

A distant voice with an Irish brogue sounded in her ears.

"You know my story. You know what to do for me."

Then the sight dissolved. Joanna was fully conscious on a bright morning in her own room. She rushed to the window. She was in her own time again.

Her mind was in turmoil. She spoke to no one through breakfast and afterwards made no attempt to see Steve. An idea which seemed crazy had formed in her mind; if she were to carry it through she could tell no one why she was doing what she intended. How she would explain herself if what she did turned out a waste of time she had no idea.

She went out to where the signpost used to be. She had fixed in her mind where the grave had been dug. Though the driveway was now tarred, little else had changed. As it had been two hundred years before, the area round the trackways was all grass.

She went back to the outhouse and selected a spade and a fork. When she returned to the crossroads she looked back at the house and then up and down the road for a sign of life. None. The farmworkers were all in faraway fields; no one in the house had time to look out of the

158

window. So, greatly daring, feeling at worst like a body-snatcher, at best just stupid, she started to dig.

She dug all morning. She laid bare a huge trench; piles of soft brown earth were heaped all round her. She found nothing. Sometimes there was a clang as the spade hit something hard. It was always a stone. At midday she went inside for something to eat; amazingly, no one questioned what she was doing. By one o'clock she was out again, burrowing wider and deeper into the ground.

At three o'clock she heard a familiar voice. Steve.

"What the hell do you think you are doing?"

Joanna looked up at him, flushed and sweating.

"You know perfectly well what I'm doing," she said.

Steve didn't answer directly.

"I've been in town all day," he said. "At the Library."

"Well?" said Joanna.

"It's true. Lanahan and James Phipps fought on Harrow's Common in May 1806. And Lanahan won. I looked it up. And it's true about Pierce Egan. I found some of his stuff. He wrote a report on the fight. Word for word what we heard. And Phipps died all right. But Egan didn't know what happened to Lanahan. Or if he did, he wouldn't say. I copied down that bit that he wrote. Listen. 'Lanahan never again graced the field of glory. Dark rumours persist about the poor fellow's end. Most likely it is that he returned to his native *Erin*, to pursue a life of honest toil among his countrymen.' Well, if Egan knew, he wouldn't say, would he?"

Joanna's spade hit something hard.

"Another stone," she said.

She cleared the earth away from it. It wasn't a stone. They both stared down as Joanna uncovered the object. It was a human skull. She dug further round, carefully. Steve took the fork and helped her.

Eventually, they saw it all. A perfect skeleton, lying straight in the soil. The neck was broken, the arms placed across the chest.

"It's him," said Steve.

Joanna choked back tears which surprised her with their force.

"He has to be buried properly," she said. "He didn't kill himself."

"We'll have to get the police. They'll be an inquest. We've got a lot of proving to do," said Steve.

"That's what he wanted; to be buried properly by his own Church," said Joanna. "It meant everything to him. Enough for us to be called back to him. We've got to make sure it's done. He trusts us."

Steve looked down at the remains of Lanahan.

Joanna continued, "And he wants forgiveness. It's got to come from you, Steve."

Steve continued to look down. There was a long silence. Then he spoke.

"We can't go holding grudges over centuries," he said. "There'll be no hope for anyone if we do. Yes, I forgive you, Lanahan. So does Jim. I'll speak for him. But can you forgive us?"

The afternoon sun shone down on the signpost, Crossways Farm and – a little away – Scratch Cottages next to Harrow's Common. Just as it had all those years ago. But, hard though Joanna and Steve listened, they heard no answer to their question.